THE FOOTPRINT

A. M. FREITAS

INDIA • SINGAPORE • MALAYSIA

ISBN 979-8-88975-529-6

This book is dedicated in loving memory of
Kurt Harris

Contents

1

Right Place/Wrong Time

Buzzz Buzzzz Buzzzz Buzzzzz Buzzzz, a phone kept vibrating as a man was about to drink his coffee.

'Ohhh Boy, this is going to be fun' He said as he attended the phone and said 'Hello'.

'Screw you Mikey, you're just a no good bastard', A woman screamed in high pitch; her voice was audible to the next table through the phone.

'Thank you, I have heard worse than this. Since you wanted the reason why I broke up with you, You have the answer, I could use less drama than your jealousy taking over every time I see a picture of a woman. I have to go Lisa, bye!' He cut the phone and shut it down.

'Women Ehhh?' Michelangelo sighed at the table nearby where a couple were staring at him subtly.

Not the first time they would have seen a drama like this played out in public in Naples, but there is always an element of curiosity which creeps the human mind when it is a couple arguing, especially when the voice of the woman is audible to the next table over the phone.

He sipped his coffee and pulled the chair nearby to the table as he sat down; the sun was shining in his face with a yellowish orange ray beaming inside the shop through the glass. It was a pleasant Saturday morning, almost the end of summer and the start of autumn. Michelangelo's phone buzzed again and he saw it was the same woman who had called earlier, he switched off the phone and started to light a cigarette. He shook his head looking at his phone and turned to his right with one sparrow getting his attention. As he sat there following its movements with a smile on his face, it soon disappeared when he heard a loud crash nearby on the road.

Screams of horror echoed as a couple of the waitresses dropped their trays, people on the road were seen running on his right. He blew the cigarette smoke out of his mouth and got up his chair and made his way quickly out the door to see what the commotion was about. The calm autumn morning seemed to turn into a stormy hailstorm within seconds by what he saw. A dead man was seen on top of a car, thrown somewhere from one of the tallest hotels under construction in the city. On closer inspection, it was found to be the owner of the hotel who was constructing the said building, Silvio Ruggeri; one of the most influential businessmen in the city, a man who isn't short of enemies, with connections on the good and the bad side as every powerful man in Italy was known for.

Michelangelo saw the body and deduced there was no way the person could have survived the fall, he pushed his way through the crowd and ran to the lift of the building, he caught hold of one of the foreman who was still trying to get the grips of what had happened in the construction of the building they were working on till then.

'Where did this happen? Which floor? Talk! Now!' Screamed Michelangelo in the face of the guy.

'We don't know exactly, but we believe it has to be either from the 23rd floor or the 24th.' The guy shivered, answering Michelangelo who had grabbed him by the collar with a firm grip while interrogating.

Michelangelo let go off the man and ran to the elevator and pressed to the top floor. He took a pair of gloves from inside his pocket as the elevator came to a halt, wearing them in each hand as he made his way into the side of the building which faced the road. He saw a group of workers rooted to a specific spot and figured he was on the correct floor, from where Silvio could have been thrown.

'Step aside and don't touch anything, I am a cop.' He ordered the three workers inside the room as he showed them his badge. They whispered among themselves, still shocked and confused as they moved to the side. The room was a bloody mess, blood spilled everywhere with a broken chair, it was getting clearly evident that Silvio was not killed quickly, the murderer had full knowledge of the building's layout. There was no other explanation which made any sense since some of the drops of blood on the wall had dried, by the looks of it, about ten hours ago, based on what Michelangelo saw. It was a public holiday in Italy, the killer took full advantage of that fact that he had the place all to himself to carry out his task with most likely half the staff not working on the building..

'Face the wall, hands on your head. How did you three come here? Where have you all been since this morning? Who else is in the building? Where are they? Who was here on this floor? Answer me!' Michelangelo asked while he pulled his gun.

"We've just come, we were all having a smoke on the ground floor when we heard the window crash and came upstairs. We were the only one's in today, the others are supposed to arrive in the afternoon,' said one of them.

'Can I see some identification? How many of you were scheduled, how many stairs are on this floor?....' Before he could finish the sentence, sirens could be heard in the background. Mike went to the next room of the building and checked from his windows, he saw the ambulances and the police had arrived. Few of them were making it to the top of the building from what he saw.

"Stay where you are and don't move! " He told the three workers as he made his way out of the entrance of the floor. He kept his gun inside his holster as he put on

his badge, Michelangelo Costa, a senior detective with AISI, Italian Intelligence.

The lift started to open and out came three police officers who came directly at Mike, he pulled his badge and waved them to back down. The officers came in and started talking to him to find out what had happened and how he had managed to be on the scene before any of them could make it.

'Am surprised only three of you are here, saw a lot more coming upstairs I assume and what's your name?' Mike asked as he looked at one of the policemen.

'Yes, we wanted to comb every entrance on the way up and you never really answered my question, Roberto would be my name!' replied the policemen.

'Think that's one for your report, but if you need to be this curious, I was having coffee in the cafe in the nearby building before the commotion outside made me get involved.' Mike responded as the other officers came up the stairs, along with a couple of forensics.

'Believe Silvio was kept here overnight and tortured, the scene in the room is not something which someone did by impulse, would you be kind enough to forward the details of your findings to my office and ask for me? Mike said while seeing the Forensics team enter the room.

'So much for following up on a case involving Silvio." Mike sighed as he lit a cigarette moving away from the officers a few feet away. He turned on his phone and went through his contacts, looking for the name of his superior, Matteo and dialled his number. The phone rang for about ten seconds before he responded.

'What is so important that you have to call even on a day to relax Mike?' Matteo said, seeming a bit annoyed.

'Yeah, Assuming you still didn't know since it happened less than an hour ago sir, our case with Silvio has a few complications regarding the investigation.' Mike said while sighing and breathing in the cigarette puff.

'Can you be more direct?' Matteo responded.

'Well Sir, he's just been murdered and it was not pretty until he was finally dead.' Mike responded while smoking.

'How, who? And how do you know all the details?' Matteo asked, trying to understand the situation further.

'Same thing I told the officers who arrived on the scene, having a coffee nearby his new luxury hotel he was constructing before he had a hard lesson in gravity by flying outside his window from the top floor. From the looks of it, the killer has already made a clean break from the building, the police are searching floor by floor, but someone who had managed to torture one of the biggest names in the city all night and kill him, don't think he would be that stupid to not have an escape plan, just saying.' He said looking blankly at all the entrances on the floor while throwing the cigarette away.

'I am coming to the office boss, I need to talk to you.' Mike said sternly.

'I know what you're going to ask Mike, meet me at my house when you're done there, I'll see what I can do.' Matteo replied. He disconnected the call.

'Great, thanks boss.' He put the phone on vibrate as he turned around.

One of the three officers who came up the escalator reached Mike while taking notes for the report. Mike was getting less than impressed, but he knew how police procedures were, part of the reason why he was on informal suspension, a forced vacation to get his mind back on track, for breaking the rules far too often. His reputation in the agency was a mixed bag, unbelievably good at solving cases, but went off the book far too many times to get things done which brought him at loggerheads with his bosses.

'How can I help you, officer?' He had a fake smile on his face while he lit up another cigarette.'

It took him close to two hours to help the officers present and to assist them with whatever he had seen and could since he was one of the first responders on scene, even if he was off duty and was supposed not be there in the first place. He took the escalator and as the doors closed, had his head rest on the side of the wall as he started shaking his head banging the wall slowly, frustration or deep in thought? He was trying to figure out how he felt about the whole situation. He walked over to his car as he took a bottle of water from inside after he opened the door. He had a few sips as he saw the scene of the murder again, the car on top of which the body had fallen down, the broken window on the top floor of the building. The entire space was already cordoned off by the police and he could see a few influential names, both on the light and dark side of the law come to the spot. He poured some water over his face as he threw the bottle into the trash can near to him.

He got inside his car and started a thirty minute drive to Matteo's house, driving around the crazy Italian traffic in the city as people were going to the beach due to it being a public holiday.

2

Back from Vacation

He screeched to a halt after driving around the city centre, getting stuck in traffic making him a bit cranky during the final streets he had to drive through. Just as he was about to hit the buzzer, the automated gates started opening. Matteo had opened the doors from inside, as he was doing some gardening. Mike parked his car a few metres away from the gate and got out of his car while lighting up another cigarette, wearing his hoodie on as the wind started blowing, rising up dust into his face.

'Good day boss.' He said as he was looking for his lighter, wiping some dust off his face as well..

'Did you even have anything to eat the whole day?' Matteo asked.

'Now that you asked, actually no and I could use a coffee.' Mike said while taking the cigarette from his mouth and keeping it in his pack.

'Let's go inside and talk.' Matteo said as he turned around to the house.

Matteo's house was close to the beach, maybe a kilometre by walk. A house he inherited from his parents, maybe the only way he could ever afford to have a house in 2022 with record levels inflation and sky high real estate prices, let alone something near the beach.

'Help yourself with the coffee, the beans are fresh, I'll be back.' He said while he went into the kitchen.

Mike started making the coffee and got two glasses from the nearby shelf. He made two double espressos for each of them and brought the cup to the table. Matteo in the meantime walked out of the kitchen bringing him a plate of Polpette and extra tomato sauce on the side. He laid the plate before Mike and took the cup of coffee which was made for him.

'Let me come to the point, you want to be back from suspension, which I forced on you as a vacation just so you don't get officially suspended for your mess up last time?' Matteo asked if he drank the coffee in one shot.

'Pretty straightforward.' Mike said as he ate a meatball, pouring the extra tomato sauce on top of his dish.

'Give me one good reason why?' Matteo asked, looking at Mike.

"Cause I am your best agent on this and don't try to say no, I've been on this case for two years, I go out for three weeks which I did. One of them is already dead and I really need to find out who and why someone killed him? Seems a fair enough reason to me." Mike said as he ate another meatball.

"Still does not negate the fact that you ended up almost killing one guy in your last arrest, even when you had specific instructions to bring him unharmed.' Matteo said.

"Jesus Christ, are we still on this? You know as well as I do, if anything, I ended up saving the life of that woman that day, he would have put a bullet in her head before we could have done anything meaningful.

Come on Sir, seriously? You know as well as I do that the official reason was bullshit and if anything, it just gave a reason for the chief to finally get back at me for getting a divorce from his daughter, you know this, everyone knows this. If anything, I have done worse than this and didn't get half in trouble like I did now." Mike said while eating more and more meatballs as he took his coffee and started sipping.

'Well I did warn you when you two were getting a divorce that this was going to bite you in the ass' Matteo said as he pulled a chair onto the table.

'What can I say, shit happened, cut to the chase, can you help me or not? I need to be back, somehow I just feel something is wrong.' Mike said frustrated at the situation.

'Of course something is wrong, Silvio is dead. Probably that's also a good enough reason to convince the higher ups to bring you back sooner than expected. Maybe him dying wasn't a bad deal for you in the grand scheme of things.' Matteo responded.

'Well that's one positive thing for the day, apart from the food you served.' Mike said while giving a grin. Matteo shook his head and rolled his eyes upon hearing what he just heard.

'Boss, I am being honest, the food was great, and so is the news that you're going to help me.' Mike said as he was wiping off the plate with his fork.

'Mike, please be serious, I want you to hold back for a day or two, I'll call you when I see the timing is right after I speak to the chief tomorrow.' Matteo said while he took the plates off the table, going into the kitchen.

'Do you need anything from my side for now?' Mike asked.

'Yeah, just take a fruit with you on the way out and get some sleep and try not to get yourself involved even indirectly in anything related to this case for the rest of the day.' Matteo said from the kitchen.

'Sure thing, thanks for having me, Sir.' Mike responded as he took a banana and let himself out of the house.

He walked over to his car while eating the fruit and turned around as he saw Matteo waving him out from the balcony on the first floor. Mike just nodded in acknowledgement as he threw the banana peel into the compost pit nearby. He got into his car and rode away, while thinking about the incident which led to his suspension.

Michelangelo Costa, born in the port city of Brindisi to Dalila and Giuseppe, Mother and Father getting divorced at a young age, Mike never really saw his Mother as she had moved out of Italy by the time he was one year old, never hearing from her. His Father, ensuring all he could to make sure Mike never missed his Mother, but fate played a cruel twist when his Father was involved in a major fire accident, in an orphanage he was working as a caretaker and perished on the spot leaving Mike to grow up in an orphanage himself. It is there he came into contact with Deputy Chief Matteo, who was a volunteer every Sunday as he attended the Church which was on the same grounds as the orphanage.

Mike having a rough childhood, showed remarkable potential and was always good at board games and puzzles, his favourite stories being crimes which Matteo solved being in the police force, his thinking was unorthodox for someone his age, as he grew up, he had a dying passion to join the police which he did, after completing his Masters in Criminology from the University of Bologna, he achieved his dream when he joined AISI, Italian Secret Services in 2010. Gaining a penchant for someone who didn't go by the rules but having an exemplary success rate in the cases he handled, Mike quickly rose up the ranks in the force, albeit with Matteo having to ensure he got him out of sticky situations with his higher bosses once a while. Mike, to his part, looked Matteo as a mentor and as his only family left, even if they were not related by blood.

In 2020, during the peak of covid lockdowns in Italy, Mike got involved in a case which would keep him occupied until now, tracking a bunch of influential people who had ties with various Italian Mafias, the ones which were threatening the internal security of the country. Rumours started to grow on two specific people, Minister of Culture, Emmanuel Trentino and influential billionaire businessman, Luca Marchesi, both being very close in the past but having a fallout at some point. Rumours had that time swirled around Luca Marchesi having a soft spot in the affairs of the foundation he was part of for the underprivileged. Their story of coming into power began with the cigarette smuggling wars beginning in the 1970's. They slowly worked their way up together before this rift caused them to go their separate ways. Maybe it was fate that someone like Luca shouldn't even be anywhere close to doing something noble to wash off his sins. None had an idea about what went wrong except multiple stories running concurrently, hard to piece together which one is true when you have a hundred different stories. During early 2021, a consignment of weapons which involved bombs being smuggled through Brindisi, with the help from the Albanian Mafia was caught by the coast guards. One of the stories which was discussed in hush circles was Emmanuel and Luca vying for control over Southern Italy. But what baffled everyone was their need to renew their rivalry with blood spill all over again, which started to be a top secret investigation with only a handful in the force knowing about this. Why would they even mention this? When the two most powerful people in the country, who had links to every politician possible and maybe even had half the authorities in their payroll.

The case took a turn about a month ago, at the end of July, Vincenzo Marchesi was found dead, his body floating over the sea covered in bullets. The obvious culprit who was looked at was Minister of Culture, Emmanuel Trentino. Vincenzo was the oldest brother in the Marchesi family and a key figure for his younger brother's rise to power, so taking him out showed a statement, the war had begun officially and the gloves were finally off after both sides were kept in chains for long.

Silvio Ruggeri was a close confidante of the Marchesi family, the murders seemed to all point towards the direction of the Trentino's, but there was no way to establish it yet. Mike knew what he was getting into when he was pulled into this team who was investigating this in the force. The shootout last month he was involved in was to arrest one of the local smugglers, Massimo, who was wanted for a shipment of smuggled gold, about a hundred kilos. Since it had the Albanian Mafia on its trail, Mike was very interested in the details on what he could dig up. what was supposed to be a routine questioning for information turned violent, one thing leading to the other with a hostage situation. Mike had ended up shooting the local fruit seller in the leg to induce shock, Massimo had let go for a split second when he was shot twice by Mike on his shoulder and his right hand, shattering his thumb in half. Massimo was brought in alive, as requested by the chief, the problem itself was the public shooting, bad press and ending up with a fallout leading to his forced vacation to act as a suspension.

Whirrrllllllllllll!!!

Mike's car swirled as he missed the oncoming truck by just a metre, the car did a couple of more swirls before he got the vehicle under control, but not before he had stuck the car into murky mud on the side of the road. He got out and noticed he had a flat tire to further add to his misery. He kicked the car door shut as he lit another cigarette.

'Yeah, I guess, I need to quit this soon, what a fucking day.', He smirked as he looked at his pack of MS, seeing the sun was going down under the trees on the road he parked in.

He was a five-minute drive away from his house and called his local mechanic for help with towing his car back home and fixing it. He put on his headphones and turned on some music as he walked home. He saw his next apartment neighbour, Rita, trying to juggle her kid and groceries on another hand. He put down his cigarette as he got the grocery bags from her as he walked them to the elevator.

'Busy day? You seem a mess.' She asked Mike.

'Lousy day for a public holiday, long story.' He smiled as the elevator came to a close on the second floor. He walked her to her door and kept the grocery bags down.

'Thanks Mike, I hope your evening is better than your day then.' Rita smiled as she got the bags and her kid in as she closed the door behind.

'Yeah I wish.' He picked his cigarette pack and was about to light one as he kept one in his mouth, he thought for a couple of seconds and decided against it and put it back into his pack as he opened the doors to his apartment.

He got his tie and shirt off and went over to the fridge, and he got himself a beer. He turned on the TV and the first thing he saw was the murder news flashing on every major news channel in the city, even National TV news channels were not far away.

'Funny how this rat bastard gets all this attention for being dead instead of actually focusing on some of his earlier crimes. Free media my ass.' Mike said as he sipped on the beer.

He looked at the time and saw it was around eight in the evening, leaving the half drunk beer at the table, Mike went into the bathroom. Turning on the water, he pulled a chair which was near the bathroom mirror and placed it right under the shower and just sat down. He shook his head left to right and looked up and down, letting the water hit his face as he put his hands over his face and moved it to his hair, just sitting there in the same position for over ten minutes deep in thought before getting up and leaving the shower.

He came out and saw that his ex-wife had texted him, wondering whether this was something to do with the broken marriage or that he had to go to the police station tomorrow and see whether he was still on suspension. He checked WhatsApp and saw that she had written in text with the message,

"Please be on your best behaviour for tomorrow at 8AM, I had to pitch for you with my dad after Matteo had called earlier." She had sent this voice note.

Mike gave a small smirk to himself knowing fully well there was drama waiting for him tomorrow once he went to the city's AISI headquarters, he wrote her back stating 'Thank You'. He found his pyjamas on the chair, put them on and made his way to bed. Saying a small prayer and putting the sign of the cross as he finished, he closed his eyes and fell asleep thinking about his day one last time.

Mike was woken by a football crashing into his window though it wasn't broken, it was loud enough for him to wake up with the glass vibrating from the impact.

'Uhh Fuck, one of these days that window is gonna break and someone's going to be in real trouble, for their own sake I really hope one of them becomes the next Francesco Totti." Mike swore as he woke up and sat down on his bed as he looked at the time on the clock on the wall. He facepalmed himself as he realised that he had missed his alarm and had woken up late. It was already 9 AM. in the morning.

He quickly got up and brushed his teeth, washed his face, brushed his hair, hurriedly changed his pyjamas to the only clean clothes he had in the closet, called a cab to his place quickly and made his way to the police precinct. He went to the station in a few minutes considering the traffic, paid the driver and got down and saw Matteo was standing outside and having a cigarette, he saw him and shook his head. Mike gave a sheepish smile as he made his way to Matteo.

"Please don't even say a word, go in and wait in my cabin." Matteo said as he continued smoking.

When inside the building, Mike saw his colleagues noticing that he had entered, Lorenzo, one of the few people that liked him and also a good friend came over and gave him a hug.

"You'd better have a good reason for being late today most of all days, the chief is really angry and I'm not sure if that is because of your attitude or because of your divorce to his daughter, but either way Matteo got some flak for you not being here at 8AM. before he went out for a smoke. But it's really good to see you here again; just try to stay out of trouble this time." Lorenzo said.

"Why do I get the feeling that it's not just me being late that pissed off the chief, what's the story running about the murder yesterday? Did we get the final report and the autopsy and all the necessary documents yet or are they still working on this?" Mike asked as he took a seat at Lorenzo's desk.

"We got all of them today morning, the only thing missing is you being assigned to this case all over again so that you can actually read them, so my advice is try not to act too smart."

"Thanks for the advice buddy, and I'm going to need your sandwich I'm starving, thank you." Mike said, and he took Lorenzo's sandwich without giving him a chance to say no.

"Dude, that's my last Iberian pork sandwich, come on Mike! Fuck you, here you might as well take my coffee as well, have the full package! I'm going to go to the vending machine and get myself a soda or something." Lorenzo said as he patted Mike on the back and walked to the vending machine, annoyed.

Mike barely took a bite of the sandwich and was about to take a sip of the coffee, when Matteo walked to Lorenzo's desk and asked Mike to follow him. He took one big bite and shot down the coffee and walked with Matteo. They entered the Director of the AISI's room, who was also Mike's ex father-in-law, Domenico Bosco. What was said in the next two minutes surprised Michelangelo.

"Take charge of the case Mike, the police reports are on your desk. This is your case now, and all I want is a resolution as soon as possible. Try to find the link between this murder and the last one; try to see if there is a pattern."

"Sure, Chief." Mike responded as he saluted Domenico and left the room with Matteo following him. " That was surprising." He added as he looked at Matteo.

"It happens when it's actually a VIP in the entire region that gets murdered, also, he already chewed me in the morning on your behalf so just get to work, and call your ex and say a big thanks." Matteo said.

Mike went to his desk but quickly took a detour back to Lorenzo's and grabbed the remaining sandwich as he made his way back to his desk and took a look at the file. In the post mortem report it was stated that there were four stabbings exactly on the right kidney before Silvio was thrown out of the building from the top floor. His lambs had collapsed due to the fall and there was brain damage before the impact on the car which again implied that Silvio was tortured all night by the killer. Some injury marks just like he had expected were well over 8 hours old, both his ankles were broken, his left elbow was dislocated and his right wrist broken, half his teeth had been pulled out, on his chest the words betrayal was branded, implying that all Silvio was painfully tortured to various degrees, before he was mercifully thrown out of the window to die.

"You might have been the only bastard who was actually happy while falling down 20 floors Silvio, wow." Mike commented as he closed the file.

"You read the file? What do you think?" asked Matteo as he signalled Mike to move to his office for privacy, as he started walking to his space with Mike following close behind carrying two separate files. They entered the room as Matteo took his seat with Mike following suit as he closed the door behind.

"Well I think someone really pissed him off, I mean, to literally torture someone for hours and in this manner, it just doesn't feel right. There seems to be a lot of history here which we really need to dig through, and I need some time. I don't think we're just dealing with some regular murder here, the fact that he was able to do this to one of the big shots in the city for hours together and the murder happening at his own property and for everyone to see, just feels like a statement here."

"Well you just said what I was thinking as well, so let's get to work, what do you need from me? If you have anything in mind that is." Matteo said as he looked at Mike intently for his opinion..

"Think it's about time we paid Alessio a visit, since he was supposed to be the last person who saw Silvio, or is anyone already checking up on this?" Mike asked Matteo.

"Yeah, Mario checked on this in the morning, the meeting never happened. We're trying to track down Alessio at the moment, and I believe you should sit this one out and leave this with Lorenzo." Matteo responded looking at Mike without blinking as if to make a point.

"Why are you afraid I'm going to do something stupid and irrational again?" Mike asked sarcastically.

"It isn't even a year Mike, most people take time to grieve you didn't, if anything you went deep into the rabbit hole and it has consumed you, to the point your marriage has fallen apart and you become even more erratic, you still get results but you become more and more erratic, and in this case with the way it's going I need you to be focused rather than erratic to prove a point. So the question is, are you able to separate your personal feelings and treat this case as a case and not a Vendetta? Matteo asked Mike.

"I don't care what others think about me, I'll cut to the chase and I'm not going to sit here and make excuses for how I have been in the past year. I want to know what you think about me at this point, if you believe that I am a liability and if you believe that I will not be able to separate my emotions from this case to my personal life. If so, tell me now and I will walk. But if you believe that I'm still the person to lead this case effectively from when I started this investigation two years ago let me know, I will take over this again and I will assist Lorenzo with Alessio, I will leave that to you boss and I would rather hear from the person who has seen me since I grew up in the Orphanage and who I've looked up to since my teenage life than actually let people who barely know me dictate that. I take responsibility for a lot of things, that's the reason why I took full responsibility for the death of my unborn son on an emotional basis, but as per the law Alessio still needs to face the light, that does not mean that I'm in that kind of an emotional wreck to not differentiate my personal feelings to my professional feelings which involves this case, specifically with the death of Silvio Ruggeri." Mike said looking at Matteo with a cold but blank honest stare, only stopping once to drink water and take a deep breath."

'Mike, Lorenzo is supposed to leave in half an hour. Make sure you join him when he leaves, welcome back, kid." Matteo said.

Mike shook his head, to acknowledge that he understood what Matteo just told him. He went outside his office, shutting the door behind him on his way out and moved towards Lorenzo's desk, who was struggling to turn on his laptop. He went over and kept the files on his desk as he took the laptop after unplugging the power cable.

"One of these days I swear to god you're gonna break this thing, I told you a million times why don't you just ask them to change the stupid battery Lorenzo? Jesus Christ!" Mike said as he removed the battery from the laptop and plugged it back on doing a power cycle on the laptop.

"I did raise a request a week ago, blame bureaucracy don't blame me." Lorenzo responded, acting aloof.

"Haven't I told you this almost a month ago before I was on a supposed vacation/suspension, I mean it must have been hard for you to actually take over some of the things for a few days without me guiding you right?"

Mike said as he plugged the laptop to the power cable and pressed the power button, the laptop turned on instantly while it was loading up the boot screen.

"I am not going to lie; I did miss you in the office, but I definitely did not miss this." Lorenzo responded, giving a grin talking about Mike's behaviour.

"So what are you supposed to do today? Do you need my assistance somewhere before I leave because Matteo told me to investigate this thing about Alessio." Lorenzo asked Mike.

"I'm coming with you, so I need you to drive and unless you literally have to take something from the laptop, I'm assuming we can leave now rather than wait for another fifteen minutes." Mike said as he started to put on his coat.

"Since when did the plan change, like how's that you come to the office only like an hour ago and already plans start to change in this case." Lorenzo said as he took his jacket from the chair.

Lorenzo took his gun from the drawer and kept it in his holster, he started buttoning his jacket as he saw Mike was already almost at the door and walking out. Mike was giving the vibe of not taking things slow especially with the name Alessio being involved and with the history behind Alessio and Mike. Lorenzo walked behind and within two minutes he was also outside in the parking lot and Mike was already there, having a cigarette. Lorenzo turned off the security of the car, and Mike got inside first. Lorenzo went into the driver's seat and did the same, Lorenzo ignited and started driving towards Casoria.

"Mike, not that you don't know already or wouldn't have thought about this a hundred times before, but are you sure you got this?" Lorenzo asked while driving straight.

"Not all scenarios can be prepared Lorenzo, this is one of them or probably on the very top of that prepared list. Then again that's why we're on the force, if a doctor thinks he can't handle emotions, he shouldn't be a doctor. If I let my emotions control me I shouldn't be on the force, so trust me I'm ok. It's my choice, I want that bitch dead, but I also know that I have the duty to find out what's happened and for the truth to come out and for that I need Alessio to find out what happened to Silvio two nights ago."

Lorenzo just nodded as he looked to the side, Mike was intently scrolling on his phone. He was looking at all the articles which were relating to Silvio's murder and was checking the reaction on social media about his death. Reactions seemed to be mixed, not as if everyone enjoyed that Silvio was dead; most of them just didn't care too much. Who could blame them; there was a recession and there were job cuts, the economy was in tatters, so a dying billionaire who probably lived a really good life until then, didn't have too much sympathy from the lower and the middle class. Although the reactions to the murder and the way it happened was shocking for everyone, in that sense, people were really interested in finding more details about this murder so it had significant press coverage and social media discussion ongoing.

"What do you think is going to happen when you find Alessio, do you really think he's going to talk?" Lorenzo asked Mike.

"Maybe, maybe not. I'm pretty much guessing not, but it doesn't mean that we need to stop trying, does it? We don't have a warrant Lorenzo, maybe we get lucky or better yet I get lucky, and I get to feed him his own teeth." Mike said while scrolling through his phone.

"Well maybe we do, maybe we don't. Can you imagine the number of crime lords who are actually happy that Silvio is dead, and at the same time there's a number of crime lords are equally scared out of their mind that he is dead." Lorenzo asked.

"I definitely see the storm, the question is who is well prepared to handle it." Mike said while keeping his phone away inside his jacket." Mike replied.

"What do you mean?" Lorenzo asked Mike.

"The same thing I told earlier is the same thing I'm telling you Lorenzo. I just can't shake the feeling that someone is making a statement here. Vincenzo Marchesi, a month ago and now Silvio. Two people at the very top of the barrel were taken down in a span of a month.

We knew what we signed up for when we took the case 2 years ago, but I assume we're going to be forced to find solutions sooner than we expected and it starts with Alessio." Mike said thoughtfully as he looked at Lorenzo.

Within the next 5 minutes, they reached the warehouse of Alessio where he operated from during the weekdays. Alessio was the muscle for Silvio in his real estate as well as other businesses, which he needed to take care of if he did not want it to be by law. Lorenzo stopped the car as Mike got out first, Alessio's loyal bodyguards Mike coming and stopped him before he could enter the office of Alessio. Mike calmly pulled out his warrant from his back, opened it and kept it a foot before the face of one of the bodyguards who stopped them to imply that by law he was allowed to go and speak to Alessio and if needed, to actually arrest him. But before Mike could proceed further, Mike noticed something was strange. He turned around and asked the other bodyguard where to find Alessio. The answer was something which Mike expected, yet he wasn't sure if he should have been surprised just because he wanted to believe it this time.

"What do you mean he has been missing since last evening? Wasn't there a meeting with Silvio which he should have been a part of?" asked Mike.

"We don't know about any meeting, I think your warrant was for Alessio, not for anyone else in this compound to talk to you." Renato, one of the bodyguards responded.

"You know I was hoping to do this to your boss, but I think I am ok with the substitute for now." Mike said as he punched Renato in the face breaking his nose, who fell on his back. The other bodyguard started coming forward and a few of the warehouse workers started gathering around. Lorenzo took his gun out as he started to keep an eye out for Mike who bent over and grabbed Renato by the neck.

"It's a pity that you have a really punchable nose and your mouth actually enables that to be highlighted like the star on a Christmas tree. Coming back to my question, where is your boss Alessio, if he is missing, where and when was he seen the last time? Has he done something which led to Silvio being murdered? Is that why he is missing and where were you idiots the entire night?!" Mike asked Renato.

"We were in Brindisi and arrived yesterday in the afternoon, this is the last time we saw Alessio, I'm not saying anything further until you get your hands off my neck, your pistol alone it's not going to stop over 20 men in this warehouse." Renato told Mike as he was looking at Lorenzo.

"Are we supposed to be afraid of this right now or you're just expecting us to walk away without getting answers? Listen shithead, you can either talk or we can keep threatening each other and start a shootout between you idiots and the police force; I mean, me and Lorenzo here might be killed, but somehow I get the feeling none of you morons here are actually getting out of here alive if that happens. So what do you say hot shot? Are you sure you want to go down that road?" Mike asked Renato showing no fear as Lorenzo held his ground.

"Let him go, I need a smoke and I wouldn't mind both of you to join me." Enzo, Alessio's right-hand man, walked from the back of the warehouse workers and stood near Mike.

Mike let go off Renato's neck and got on his feet as he turned around and nodded at Lorenzo, who in turn kept his gun on his holster. Enzo started walking towards another part of the warehouse far away from all the people. Mike and Lorenzo followed them behind keeping a close eye on proceedings. Enzo stopped near a forklift which was parked near blocks of wood, presumably which was supposed to be used on the construction that took place in the property.

"I'm not going to waste your time Mike, Alessio is indeed missing and I don't think he had anything to do with Silvio's murder." Enzo said as he lit up a cigarette.

"Enzo, really you brought me up all this way, like fifty metres maybe? Just to give me this answer, come on man, even if I want to believe you, give me one good reason why I should actually trust you on this?" Mike asked Enzo.

"Cause that's the truth Mike, I can only tell you what I know and I can only tell you that our men are looking for Alessio and ever since we knew about Silvio's murder, our men have actually been tracking Alessio without any clues where he is. So spare me the pleasantries and unless you have any details about Alessio I would suggest you to leave." Enzo told Mike and Lorenzo.

"Okay, but I'm going to need a couple of details from you before I leave. Somehow I get the feeling that you need your boss as much as I do at this point. So what do you say we try to help each other here for once? Even if I actually want your boss to rot in hell at this very moment, I kind of need him alive, so what do you say that we actually play ball together this time, huh?" Mike told Enzo, who thought for a while before he started talking.

"Alessio left for Portici in the afternoon, and he had changed the meeting from here to the place where he was. Since this involved Silvio he requested to be left alone which I did, but ever since we saw and heard about the murder of Silvio, we were trying to track down Alessio who went missing pretty much at the same time. So your guess is as good as mine Mike. Is Alessio alive? I don't know and that's what we're trying to find out as well. As I said earlier, unless you actually have any news about this I would expect you to leave." Enzo told both Mike and Lorenzo again.

"For your own sake Enzo, I do hope that is the truth. Either way, we will always have an eye on you all, and don't forget to send a telegram or a pigeon carrying a note when you find your boss." Mike said as he turned around and walked to the car.

"One piece of advice, Enzo, I hope you guys don't make it more personal than it already is for him. Just to reconfirm, the warehouse in Portici, right?" Lorenzo said while taking his sunglasses and wearing them.

Enzo just stood there staring at Lorenzo, who took the silence as a yes and turned around, heading to the car. He got inside the car while Mike was busy making notes on his phone. Lorenzo put on his seatbelt and started the car, started to back off and drive out of the warehouse.

3

The Mystery Continues

"Are you ok buddy?" Lorenzo asked Mike.

"Yeah, just thinking whoever this guy might be, if he managed to take down Alessio and Silvio on the same night. Balls man, guy has balls I'll give him that." Mike said as he kept his phone aside.

"Seems to me he has your attention." Lorenzo said to Mike.

"Well how long have we been trying to put these guys in court, things have never really worked in our favour, did it? Not that I care about Silvio but if something did happen to Alessio, I'm just going to say karma. Still I'm going to do my duty as the cop and hopefully try to recover him if he is still breathing and then ask what happened." Mike said to Lorenzo with a casual chuckle.

"Seriously what do you think, jokes aside Mike." Lorenzo asked Mike again.

'If you want my honest opinion, I don't think Alessio is alive or even if he is, not for long. Our guy is leaving a statement for something. Look at it this way: the three people he has touched in the past month are not some random persons on the street. He's practically taking out the people who own the district. This is going to get ugly, the question is if we are going to take the dirt on our faces as well." Mike said as he looked at Lorenzo.

"Let me call someone to check the warehouse in Portici." Lorenzo said.

"I already did that while you were coming back to the car; I also called Matteo and informed them of what Enzo said. Let's just go back to the station; I think, we need to come up with a proper plan so let's discuss this with Matteo and the team and take this further." Mike told Lorenzo who just shook his head and looked at the road.

They were there at the station in another twenty minutes. Mike and Lorenzo got down from the car and proceeded to the main building. They noticed Federico, one of the guys in the team, running inside hurriedly and at the same moment, both Mike and Lorenzo received text notifications on their phone. Mike stopped and checked his phone as Lorenzo stopped two steps further to Mike and took his phone out as well. Lorenzo flailed his arms as if in shock and disgust, Mike saw the message and just shook his head biting his tongue.

"Holy fuck, I wish my predictions would come true for the lottery, let's go. Atleast worth a million bucks then" Mike said to Lorenzo as he started running to the main building, who followed him close behind.

They entered the door and saw a huge commotion at the station. A lot of eyes were glued to the TV monitors hanging on the walls. Images of a dead Alessio's body being recovered from the ocean were shown, the murderer had left the body mutilated the same way Silvio was tortured. Mike noticed Domenico and Matteo having a discussion with other senior officers on the other side of the room, inside Domenico's office room. He went over and tried to join in on the conversation and see if he could be of any use. He turned the knob of the door, opened it slowly and gave a wave for Domenico and Matteo to see and walked right in.

"Three murders in one-month, I don't think we had this many big heads rolling even when there were full blown mafia wars and bomb blasts around the country. Vincenzo, Silvio and now Alessio, who's next?" Domenico fumed.

"Matteo and Michelangelo, this is your case which you both started the investigation two years ago, what do we have? Do we have any leads into these murders? Is this even something related to the investigation we have been on in the first place, it's like I ordered coffee and I got green tea in cold water. I got a couple of cabinet members on my ass after these images flashed on TV." He fumed further.

"Myself and Lorenzo went to Alessio's warehouse, as I detailed earlier before coming back to the station.

Alessio didn't seem to hide as we thought. Enzo, his trusted aide, confirmed Alessio was missing since the time he was supposed to meet Silvio. The place of the meeting was also changed at the last minute, so they were searching for him as well for the past two days." Mike pitched in with whatever he knew to Domenico.

"With your permission sir, I would like to go to the hospital and look at the body and be present during the autopsy." Mike further added.

"Go." Domenico answered.

"Do we know anything else, Mike?" Matteo asked.

"Nothing yet sir, still digging through details and piecing stuff together." Mike responded.

"This was supposed to be a secret investigation; the five people in this room, the one guy on his honeymoon, are the only ones dealing with this entire investigation. With all these folks then, how is that possible people in our watch can just drop dead at the moment?!" Domenico said and drank a glass of water, seemingly to calm himself.

"So do you believe that one of us is a mole?" Federico asked, surprised.

"No, Federico, that is not what I'm implying, but I am saying that maybe, during the investigation in the past two years there was something which we missed. So maybe it is not a bad idea for all of you to figure this out.

Find the missing pieces from the past two years! Is this something related to any mafia which we are missing out on?" Domenico asked.

"Sir, if I may add, in the past 2 years whatever we hoped to achieve was to bring the illegal activities of all these people to light. We have established a pattern on their smuggling ring, money laundering and other illegal businesses. My problem here is, this has been the norm for decades. This just seems too sudden, this just feels like an old grudge not something related with business or disagreements." Mike responded.

"Mike, why don't you go to the hospital to check the body and get the autopsy reports and give us a full picture tomorrow morning? Whatever you could find and whatever you could piece together from the past two years and, Federico please accompany Mike on this." Matteo said to both Mike and Federico.

Both Mike and Federico acknowledged Matteo and left the room, they didn't say anything to each other and just kept walking to their respective cabins. Federico started to open a drawer and was intently searching through a bunch of paper. Mike, on the other hand, just went to his desk, picked up his sunglasses and started working outside of the building. Federico seemed to have found what he was looking for as he took a couple of papers from a file, folded them and kept them inside his jacket as he also made his way out of the building. Mike waited outside as he lit up a cigarette and calmly smoked while waiting for Federico to come out. As he saw Federico, Mike offered him a cigarette but Federico declined, taking a pack of chewing gum from inside his pocket.

"The day gets crazier by the minute." Federico said to Mike as he popped a couple of pieces of chewing gum inside his mouth.

"Well, I wish I had seen you out for a beer rather than see you in the office after many weeks trying to find the autopsy report of a scumbag. Although, I'm not sure which one I should be more surprised about, you declining a cigarette or Alessio being dead. Also I'm going to need you to drive Alfred Pennyworth." Mike said as he started working towards the parking lot.

"What happened to your car?" Federico asked Mike as he followed him.

"Freak accident yesterday, should be able to collect it from my mechanic on my way home today." Mike responded to Federico.

They both reached Federico's car and got into it. Federico started the engines and started driving towards The US naval hospital in Naples which depending on traffic would be about half an hour's drive from the station. Federico tried to talk to Mike and give him the details, which Mike had texted them earlier to find while he was at Alessio's Warehouse along with Lorenzo.

"I didn't really get too much headway in finding out what made Alessio to change the meeting spot, especially at the last moment." Federico said to Mike.

"Well now I know that you're useless in two languages." Mike responded to Federico.

"I knew you would say that but at least I knew what they were going to talk at this meeting mostly, this started to brew in the past five to six weeks ever since you were on your unofficial suspension as well." Federico said to Mike.

"What are you talking about? What did I miss?" Mike asked with a bit of curiosity.

"Migrants, illegal migrants coming on boats to Italy." Federico said to Mike.

"Isn't this something which we were already investigating and tied in with Vincenzo Marchesi? Please tell me you actually have a follow-up to add on top of whatever you just said." Mike replied to Federico sarcastically.

"Of course I do Mike, come on, give me some credit here. So Alessio and Silvio were trying to discuss work for illegal migrants. Now from what I can understand Vincenzo was planning to use the illegal migrants for his political stand, but Alessio and Silvio had other plans and they did have some disagreements over this. Before he was murdered, there is a good possibility that this meeting could be a follow-up on that topic, but until now the only disagreement which we know for a fact was in relation to jobs. Legally and illegally and using the mafia in all of Southern Italy to have a handle on the job situation." Federico responded to Mike as he kept his eye on the road.

"Since the elections are next year, he could have genuinely been trying to show a good face and gain brownie points with the people and the European Union. That makes it easier if whatever you said was true to narrow down the options." Mike said while looking at Federico.

"My biggest question and all this is the mafia coming into all this, which ones are getting involved because if the mafias are already involved? That could explain the murders which are happening right now. The way the killings are going, are we dealing with one single hitman or a group of hitmen targeting multiple people? Mike continued further while scratching his head.

"This is going to be a long case, I see." Federico responded looking at Mike.

"No I was mentally prepared for that since the past two years." Mike said and he put on his sunglasses and pushed back the seat to imply he was going to get some rest for the next few minutes until they reached the hospital.

Federico drove for another ten minutes as they reached the US naval hospital in Napoli, where he saw multiple police cars in the precinct. Federico tapped on Mike's shoulder to wake him up. Mike woke up and got the recliner of the seat, as the security at the gates stopped to check who they were. Mike and Federico showed their respective badges as the security let them in. They were also pointed towards where they could Park as Federico drove his car towards the point area. Both of them got out of the car and they made their way to the chief doctor's office, Martino, who seemed to have been expecting them.

"You are the officers who are dealing with the case of Alessio, I assume?" Martino asked, looking at Federico and Mike.

"Yes doctor, I'm Federico Biraghi, this would be my colleague Michelangelo Costa, do we have the initial analysis of what happened?" Federico introduced themselves and asked Martino.

"The full autopsy report should be available in a few days but the initial diagnosis you asked for is brutal." The doctor replied.

"Could you explain a bit further, doctor? Define brutal and do we have an estimated time frame when the murder could have happened and what probably gave the final blow?" Mike asked Dr Martino.

"Multiple stab wounds, finger amputations on his left hand, both his arms were broken, there were blows on his body which induced a few broken ribs. Probable cause of murder was a punctured lung and being thrown into the ocean. Again this is just the initial diagnosis we will be able to give the full picture only when we get the final reports. But the punctured lung, that is the killer blow. You may see the body if you want to, gentlemen." Dr Martino said to Federico and Mike.

"That would be nice if you could just lead the way." Mike responded to the doctor as he opened the door for him.

"Please follow me, gentlemen." Dr Martino said as he walked out of the room closely followed by Mike and Federico.

Dr Martino led them to the elevator and got inside, Mike and Federico got in as well as the Doctor on the first floor three. Before the door closed, two policemen stopped the door from closing and got in. It seemed like they were going to floor three as well as they saw the light on the buttons and just stayed idle. The elevator started and rose to the set floor in a few seconds. Mike, being curious, struck up a conversation with the policemen.

"What brings you guys to the hospital?" Mike asked one of the policemen who looked middle-aged.

"A murder, Alessio. We were there at the murder scene and brought the body to the hospital. Just going upstairs to finish the report after speaking to the doctors." The policeman replied.

"And who would you be?" The other policeman asked.

"Michelangelo Costa, Italian secret service, AISI. We're working on this case so it's great that both of you were in the murder scene. Saves time, so if I may look into your documentation already and if you could also explain to me what had happened at sea, it'll be easier for me and my colleague here too to proceed. The reason being the report you're writing right now, this most likely is going to end up in my desk either way by tomorrow, so it saves time and trouble." Mike said with a grin.

The elevator door opened as everyone inside started getting out. Dr Martino led the way to the autopsy room. In the meantime, Mike started asking further questions to the two policemen as Federico took his notebook and started taking further notes based on the conversation.

"Give me a short summary of how the body was found." Mike asked one of the policemen.

"The body was found about seven kilometres from the beach and was spotted by a fishing boat who in turn informed the police." The policeman answered.

"What time did the fishing boat find the body? How long did it take for you people to reach there?" Mike asked the policeman.

"All this happened around 7:30 in the morning, where we from the police department were there within the next thirty minutes, the body was brought to the shore around 8:30AM and we reached the hospital by 9AM. Everything is further documented in the report Mr Michelangelo." The policeman replied.

Dr Martino in the meantime had led them to the autopsy room, he invited all of them to come inside with him. All of them went outside following his lead and they reached Alessio's body. Mike went a bit closer to Alessio's body, removed the sheet a bit and saw the extent of the injuries which caused his death. The results from first glance were brutal, Mike was trying to piece the images from Silvio's murder scene to the injury marks on Alessio's and was trying to figure out which one was worse.

"Can you give me and my colleague a few minutes alone." Mike said as he looked at the policeman and Dr Martino.

Dr Martino nodded his head and left without saying a word. The two policemen on the other hand looked at each other and looked at Federico who just pointed towards the door with just a look in his eyes, while scratching his forehead with Mike staring at them on the other side. They also left after seeing the reaction of both Mike and Federico.

"No wonder our police department is a joke sometimes." Mike said as he continued to look at Alessio's injury marks in his body while Federico was reading through the notes of the autopsy which was nearby.

"This looks bad Mike, the extent of the torture, wow." Federico said while reading the notes and shaking his head.

"You heard about the saying Federico? Do those sins catch up with you eventually? I guess our boy just had his day in the sun." Mike said, looking at Alessio's face.

"I would have loved to see this bastard behind bars and spending his days in prison where half the population don't really like him, also for my dead unborn son. If I'm speaking emotionally as a person and a father, I'm just going to say justice is served. Although, it makes our case even more complicated. With all the enemies these guys have made over the past few years, we have a lot of names to go through to narrow down who is taking them down at rapid speed. Like the chief said, three big names within a month, especially two of them within a day of each other. Whoever is doing this or whatever gang is involved, they got a score to settle and this has been a long time in the making, it's getting evident by the injury marks they're leaving behind on all of these guys." Mike added further to Federico.

"So what is our next move here?" Federico asked, looking at Mike.

"I'm still processing and trying to figure that out, Federico. How many names do we have on our list, thirty? I think we really need to review that list all over again. Let's start with finding out where each and every one of them in that list has been in the past two days, whatever phone call we tapped for the past year, whichever dirtbag we arrested were linked with these assholes, we need to also have a conversation with them. Let's see if we get lucky somewhere. I'll just do a hail Mary on that for now."

"Do you think maybe we should recruit more people into this investigation?" Federico asked Mike.

"Why? Do you think that this is going to overwhelm us or what's your point? Mike questioned Federico.

"No, I just feel that it wouldn't be bad to have maybe two more heads to do the brainwork. This is still Matteo's case, so it's still got to be his final word, but I believe you will have a say in it as well that's why I'm suggesting it." Federico replied to Mike.

"Let's stick to ourselves for now, especially without knowing what kind of rabbit hole we're going in." Mike responded to Federico.

"It's your decision buddy. Who do you think we're going to release Alessio's body to?" Federico asked Mike.

"Considering this dirtbag doesn't have any family, I wouldn't be surprised if Enzo were here shortly to collect this filth." Mike responded coldly.

"Why don't you go back to the station and give whatever details we collected here at the hospital to Domenico and Matteo? I think, I'll stay here for a while and I think it's about time I had a conversation with

Enzo more privately, given the circumstances." Mike said further to Federico.

"Roger that, I'll see you tomorrow then." Federico said as he exited the room.

Mike waited until Federico had left, then he turned around, looked at Alessio's body and went over to it. He covered the face with the extra sheet and made his way out of the room as well. Mike took out his cell phone and looked for Enzo's contact details. He dialled his number; it rang five times before Enzo attended the phone call.

"I don't believe I need to be the guy who breaks the bad news, how long do you think it is going to take you to reach the hospital?" Mike asked Enzo over the phone.

"I'm already here and I'm going upstairs." Enzo responded to Mike over the phone. Mike disconnected the phone and took a seat right outside the autopsy room, and within a few minutes Enzo arrived outside the elevator along with four other men. He said something to the people following him and they kept their distance and stayed back while Enzo made his way to Mike near the autopsy room.

"Tell me, do you have something for me, Mike?" Enzo asked as he took a seat right next again near the autopsy room's waiting area.

"I do, if you decide to help me." Mike responded to Enzo.

"Decide to help you how? What do you exactly need from me? You ask us if we're best buddies, I have sympathy for you but don't mistake that for friendship or even respect." Enzo said to Mike.

"You know why I like you Enzo? Because I don't. I only care about your stupid boss's murder, and I'm trying to find out who's next on the list. I sure as hell hope it isn't you." Mike responded to Enzo.

"I pity the guy who's going to come after me, Mike, if I am indeed next on this list." Enzo defiantly replied to Mike.

"Let's leave the macho talk aside for a few minutes Enzo, you can sit here and keep giving these speeches, who knows maybe you'll get lucky and you get the murderer or that person gets lucky and puts a bullet in your head! Judging by what this guy has done to Alessio and two other people, I get the feeling having a bullet in your head isn't the worst way to go, if that is your last day on this planet. So what's it going to be, are you going to act like all macho gangster with me? Or are you going to act like a person with common sense?" Mike said to Enzo.

Enzo got up from his chair and went inside the autopsy room where Alessio's body lay. Having removed the sheet and looked at Alessio's body fully, carefully examining every injury mark, Enzo started cracking his knuckles as a way to relieve tension. The more he looked at Alessio's body, the more he was going into a silent rage. Mike stood at the entrance, leaning on the door, watching Enzo's reaction silently. Enzo saw that Mike was looking at them and covered Alessio's body with the sheet and went outside the room again, went near the window opposite of the autopsy room door and looked outside.

"Great view right?" Mike asked Enzo as he stood next to him.

"Yeah, not bad for something close to the mortuary." Enzo responded as he turned his head to the left to look at Mike.

"So tell me Enzo, you're planning to keep talking as a gangster or might let an officer who doesn't go by the rules to find out what you're also trying to find out?" Mike asked Enzo.

"I don't know what you're talking about Mike." Enzo responded indifferently to what Mike said.

"It's ok Enzo, I will wait to see if you will ever talk about Alessio's death being somehow related to Vincenzo, just try to stay alive, ok?." Mike responded with indifference as well.

"I believe it's time for you to leave Mike, this is not your fight and we will make sure this is never your fight. I need you to leave, Captain, and leave things as it is for now." Enzo said to Mike as he patted him on a shoulder and lifted his left arm towards the hallway, encouraging Mike to start walking.

Enzo's men also saw his hand raise, as they started walking over towards him. Mike sensed the situation and just smiled as he turned around and started walking the other way. He took the stairs rather than the elevator and as he was walking he slipped his fingers under the collar of his coat. Mike I was able to find a small piece of paper slipped under there and it read with the words, "Stay home at 7PM today." He had sensed that Enzo had slipped something earlier when he patted him on his shoulder, followed by a nod to imply to just follow through. Mike looked at the watch on his hand and noticed the time was close to 5PM. He started out walking outside the hospital as he was checking his phone, he noticed that he had got a message from a mechanic stating that the car had been parked outside this apartment and the keys had been given to his neighbour, Rita, who normally Mike seeked help from whenever he had a delivery or something to be collected on his behalf.

"Saves a trip, I guess." Mike said to himself as he started walking towards the bus stop.

He waited at the stop for about 5 minutes as the bus towards this area rolled by. He got inside and noticed that the bus driver was a friendly face he had known for a few years. Mike smiled as he stood next to the driver's cabin; the driver noticed Mike and gave a wave and a smile.

"Luigi, finishing your shift or starting one? How long has it been, six to seven months since we last saw each other?" Mike asked Luigi.

"I would say close to a year, I think the last time I saw you was in church, I haven't really seen you in a while there, is everything ok?" Luigi asked Mike.

"I know, I think I'm having a love and hate relationship with God, I'll be there when the hate relationship stops. For now I'm ok." Mike replied to Luigi.

"Testing times is when you should actually be seeking his advice, my friend." Luigi smiled as he kept his eyes on the road while responding to Mike.

"I know Luigi, I know, come on. I grew up in a church orphanage. It's pretty much all I was told every day until I left, so believe me, I know. We're still humans, I guess our feelings do change once in a while and it's normal." Mike quipped back at Luigi.

"Not in the faith in our Lord, my friend, not in the Lord." Luigi responded.

"I've never lost faith, I'm just taking a break. How's Matilda? Is she still working at the supermarket?" Mike asked Luigi.

"She loves the job and is still working there." Luigi responded to Mike.

"Still the simple woman who finds happiness in the smallest things, just the way I remember seeing her the last time." Mike replied to Luigi with a smile.

"She hasn't changed a bit ever since I met her Mike, this was 20 years ago." Luigi replied back to Mike.

"I think I'll get off at the next stop, Luigi, just going to grab something to drink on the way home. It was good seeing you today again." Mike said to Luigi as he pressed the door button on the bus.

"It was a pleasure Mike, I hope to see you at church sometime, maybe next time you will get over your love and hate relationship with Him." Luigi said to Mike with a smile as he waved him out of the bus."

"Hopefully, hopefully Luigi, I'll see you around and take care." Mike waved back at Luigi as he got down the bus.

Mike was about half a kilometre away from his house, he walked towards a specialty liquor store and got two bottles of Scotch. He carried the bottles in a bag as he put on his headphones and started playing some music. He kept checking his messages and noticed Rita had written to him, saying she would be leaving the house around 6PM. and requested Mike to come to pick up the keys before then if possible. Mike looked at the watch and noticed that he had maybe another fifteen minutes before 6PM. He responded to her message stating that he was on his way and he would meet her at her apartment in the next few minutes.

Mike kept walking through the streets and reached his apartment building in ten minutes and made his way to Rita's apartment. He pressed the doorbell and Rita opened the door all dressed up, as if for an event. She had Mike's car keys in her hands.

"Party or a date?" Mike asked Rita as he got his keys.

"Get your mind out of the gutter Mike." Rita responded to Mike as she got out of her door and locked it, as Mike started walking back to his apartment.

"You never gave me an answer Rita." Mike said as he opened the door and was going inside his apartment.

"Let's call it a meeting for now Mike." Rita smiled as she walked down the stairs disappearing out of Mike's sight.

"Good luck." Mike said with a raised voice and his words echoed in the stairway as he closed his door behind.

Mike kept the two bottles of Scotch on the table as he removed his jacket and threw it on the couch. He started to unbutton his shirt as he went to the window to have a look outside. He saw Rita going to her car, texting on her phone. She was smiling as she stood for a few seconds, before keeping the phone in her bag and getting into her car. Mike saw her drive away out of the apartment complex onto the main road, he nodded and gave a sigh but with a smile.

"At least someone's having a good week." Mike said to himself as he went to the fridge and got himself a beer.

Mike went to the couch and threw his jacket to the side, he took the TV remote control and tuned in to Netflix and started watching a half-finished movie as he saw the time on the clock near the bedroom wall. He opened the beer as he lay down on the couch and started watching TV while sipping the drink slowly. He turned on the volume a few points higher; he kept a remote on the table when the door was kicked open and all of a sudden two people entered the room and started shooting at Mike, before he had a chance to react.

4

HELLO ENZO

Trrrriiinnggggg trrrriiinnnggggg triiinnnggggggg

The doorbell rang, Mike woke up and noticed that he was just dreaming as he touched his chest as he gave a deep breath. The doorbell rang again; Mike checked the time, it said 7PM. He knew who was outside the door, he got up from the couch as he picked up his gun and kept it at his back and let his shirt down. He opened the door and there stood Enzo.

"May I come in?" Asked Enzo, looking at Mike when he opened the door.

"I don't think you slipped a note into my jacket to ask me this question Enzo, so please." Mike said as he waved his hand to Enzo to go inside the apartment.

Enzo entered, put his jacket on the coat stand and took a seat in the chair beside the TV. Mike picked one of the Scotch barrels and came close to the table where Enzo was sitting, placing it in the middle. Then he went to the fridge and took some ice from the freezer, put them in a bowl, picked up two glasses and brought them to the table as well. Mike opened the bottle, poured the drink on both the glasses and put a cube of ice on one of them and started sipping while he went to the couch leaving the other glass next to Enzo.

"Feel free to take some ice, or not. Now, what do you have for me Enzo?" Mike asked.

"About your question at the hospital, before I come to that, I want to know what you know from your side? What connection do you see between the murders of Vincenzo, Silvio and Alessio?" Enzo shot back at Mike as he picked his glass of Scotch and started drinking it neat.

"I can think of a few reasons a scumbag politician's brother would be on the hit list, but apart from the supposed connection in regards with the migration crisis, I can't really think of any specific reasons from my side. That's pretty much my investigation as of now Enzo, maybe that's why I wanted to talk to you. If you help me with some scraps, maybe I might be able to make it into a meal. The real question is, are you willing to give me something or we're both just wasting our time? If yes, feel free to finish the drink and get out of the door if you don't have anything to say." Mike responded, staring coldly at Enzo.

"Keeping the elections in mind for next year, Vincenzo had wanted Alessio and Silvio to tone down the operation in a few cities." Enzo said to Mike.

"What do you mean by operation, so the rumours are true Alessio was not just the muscle behind the smuggling business, he was also the overwatch for illegal migrants being used as bonded labour in Southern Italy? Or am I missing something?" Mike questioned Enzo further, trying to see if he could pull more words out of him.

"Where do you think Southern Italy keeps getting its cheap labour from to work on the agricultural fields, all the cleaning, the hard construction and everything along those lines, don't pretend you don't know Mike?" Enzo responded to Mike sipping his Scotch.

"It's not about me knowing, it's about me trying to understand where you all fit into this and how this could have put a marker on all of you." Mike said to Enzo.

"Scraps Enzo, feed me the scraps properly." Mike reiterated to Enzo as he kept sipping into his drink.

"On another day I would have cut my fingers off first before telling you what I'm about to tell now. I'm well beyond that phase anyway." Enzo sighed as he poured another round of Scotch into his glass.

"Enough for the suspense already, get on with the blasted story." Mike responded indifferently.

"I would still watch your tone if I were you Mike, I might need your help. I'm not dependent on it, I'm here because I feel I'm a part of the reason you lost your son. Nothing more nothing less." Enzo responded to Mike.

"Noted." Mike replied, biting his teeth as he held his glass tight, almost to the point of cracking it. A sense of power play on display between the two.

"Vincenzo was gunning for a seat at the parliament in the next election along with his brother, Claudio, he knew he couldn't actually do it without taking a moderate stand, politically. The major one at play is the migration crisis in Italy from Africa. Labour exploitation, prostitution and drug trafficking, using illegal migrants who have no papers and no rights whatsoever for this is a no-brainer." Enzo said to Mike as he finished his second round.

"I am still trying to understand how illegal migrants was supposed to help Vincenzo or Claudio for the cabinet chair, when he himself is involved and is one of the major players in South Italy for all these illegal activities in the first place." Mike asked Enzo.

"Mike, you playing dumb to get answers from me really isn't working." Enzo responded, making a hand gesture near his head showing his annoyance.

"Ok let's do it this way: Vincenzo has long been accused of using migrants as bonded labour for his own activities. What is it? Five journalists who have been murdered until now. The last one was seven months ago, who had written that article, Tomato Fields and migrant blood? And car accidents again, at least try not to make it so obvious it's you idiots." Mike responded as he poured another round of scotch on his glass.

"Impressive!." Enzo nodded as an acknowledgement whilst sipping his drink.

"So do you mind filling me up on the details I missed out?" Mike responded to Enzo.

"Vincenzo wasn't gunning for the post because he could, he needed it to save his life along with Claudio. Let's just say that he wasn't on the best of terms with the Albanian mafia who, along with the Trentino family, wanted them dead, it should give them full control over Southern Italy. So he decided to up his game. Vincenzo didn't just want control of Southern Italy he wanted to extend borders further and wanted to take the Albanian mafia and the Trentino family head on; he wanted full control of the entire country, the mafia's included and the only way to make that happen was to run the country himself. He's made a lot of enemies as you know over the decades, he needed further power and protection to consolidate his hold on affairs." Enzo said to Mike.

"What made the Marchesi's and Trentino's to cross paths again? I don't get it, these guys kept it together taking Central Italy and Southern Italy as borders for themselves. So why now? What does it have to do with the Albanian mafia here? Also, is it true that Vincenzo was murdered on the say-so of the Trentinos? Is this why Claudio is running in next year's elections as well? To have Emmanuel in striking distance?" Mike asked Enzo.

"That's one of the many reasons. Claudio is hell-bent and wants revenge for the death of his brother, he wants to take down the entire organisation. If he succeeds, he controls the entire country, not just South or Central Italy. it's all coming down to geography, Mike. But for this to happen he needs a reputation, this is why he had asked Silvio and Alessio to keep the activities from not reaching mainstream news. It didn't sit well too much with Alessio and Silvio, because this was a major revenue generator. Bringing down this activity by even a few per cent, they feared they would lose control over the gangs who worked on their behalf, which new players could challenge their authority. This was the reason why Vincenzo was having problems with Alessio and Silvio. With Vincenzo murdered, Claudio came in but the problems remained. Before we know it, Silvio and Alessio are dead, probably almost on the same day. Now we could blame the Trentinos or their associated circle but at this point, I wouldn't trust Claudio either." Enzo said to Mike.

"So you're saying Claudio could be the reason behind Alessio and Silvio's murder?" Mike looked at Enzo while pouring himself another drink looking for an answer.

"I didn't say that, I'm just not ruling out that option. You wanted me to give you whatever I knew, there you have it now." Enzo looked at Mike as he took the bottle from the table and poured himself another drink.

Just as Enzo made himself comfortable under the chair after getting the drink, the window glass shattered and within a split second Mike's hands had some blood splatter on it. Enzo fell forward on the table. Mike immediately fell down on the floor, turned off the lamp in the room and brought the light down as much as possible. He took his pistol and he tried to look outside the window looking for spots where the shot came from. Mike could triangulate two buildings a few hundred metres away, he dropped down the drapes to completely cover the windows and leave no line of sight from the outside to the inside of the room. Mike scrambled over to Enzo how to check for a pulse, unfortunately there was none. Enzo was dead, Mike saw a clean exit wound for the bullet on Enzo's head, he saw a bullet mark on the wall close by to Enzo's chair. He got his phone and made a call to Matteo to tell him the news of what happened.

"Hello Mike, I wasn't expecting your call this late to talk about what happened at the hospital. Do you have something for me?" Matteo asked Mike as he picked up the phone. He was also wary, when he heard Mike's footsteps hard on the ground and Mike breathing heavily, he realised Mike was running fast while on the phone.

"Mike what happened, where are you? Are you ok?" Matteo questioned further, trying to understand what was happening.

"Sorry to be the bearer of bad news, Enzo just got assassinated in my house. I don't know if it's our guy or someone else; I'm going towards the building which I believe the shot came from. I need you and the force to come to my location and my building soon." Mike said to Matteo.

"Assassinated? What? How? What was Enzo doing in your house?" Matteo asked Mike, surprised and trying to make sense of the situation.

"Matteo, I'll explain when you're here, just make it here soon, call the force and come to my house and make it to my location, Pronto!" Mike screamed back as he disconnected the phone and ran through traffic towards the next building.

He almost got run over by a car and hit a pedestrian who was walking in his mad dash, a trance-like state towards one of the buildings he assumed the shot came from. Mike stood at the entrance and was looking on all sites to see if someone suspicious was getting in his eye. He made a dash to the next building twenty metres away, checking the corners between the two buildings as he stood at the entrance of the next one and looked around.

Mike saw a couple smoking outside the building. They had also noticed Mike earlier when he had reached the earlier building, looked around and had run to the current building looking around. It was evident by the look they were giving that they were talking about Mike earlier. They were getting visibly uncomfortable as Mike ran to them. The couple started backing away, going away, throwing down their cigarettes and moving away from the location.

"Hey!! Stop right there." Mike screamed at a high pitch, as the couple froze, that man turned around as Mike ran towards them.

"Listen we don't want any trouble." The man attempted to defuse the situation, assuming Mike was a crazy person or someone about to mug them.

"I am a cop, did you see anyone come outside this building or even that one in a hurry in the past fifteen minutes, anyone? Men, women, teenagers? Anything you remember? Anything suspicious or anyone suspicious walking around here carrying a luggage or suitcase, anything at all?!" Mike asked the man, who was still confused by whatever he heard and the way Mike looked at them, trying to grasp his words.

"I didn't see anything, we just stood outside the building; we were about to go upstairs." The man responded.

"How about you, did you see someone?" Mike asked the girl.

"No, like he said we just arrived five minutes ago." She responded to Mike.

Mike started to look around the street and found there were euro to CCTV cameras nearby.

One located in the traffic light and the next one on a street lamp right behind him. Mike also noticed fresh tires screeches on the road; it looked as if someone had left in a hurry. Mike took his phone from his pocket, took some pictures of the tire marks and dialled Federico. The phone started to ring on Federico's side and it was attended after two rings.

"On my way Mike, I've asked the local police to show up at your place already. Our team should be there in the next fifteen minutes as well." Federico informed Mike as he attended the phone call without Mike saying a word.

"Yeah that's great, but I think our killer just got away." Mike responded to Federico.

"What do you mean, how do you know?" Federico asked, perplexed.

"It means that that person got away, because I think I'm standing right next to wherever they were parked at." Mike said to Federico.

"Got away? Wait, who is at your apartment?" Federico asked Mike.

"No one, Except Enzo's dead body and a locked door for the police to break into." Mike responded as he was still looking around.

"What am I supposed to do, wait until you idiots show up and wait for the potential assassin to get away? Watch the goddamn road and drive here soon." Mike replied to Federico as he disconnected the call while sending him his exact location over WhatsApp.

Mike went to the first building he had stopped at before he ran to the couple earlier and looked up. He turned around and looked at the apartment he was living in. He looked to his right and saw the next building. As Mike was looking for any open windows, and he found quite a few, the shot could have been fired from any one of them. He turned around and started walking back to his apartment as he heard Sirens. Mike heard four police cars buzzing past him on the road nearby driving towards his building. Mike clicked his tongue and started walking again. He observed two more cars and a van arriving from the opposite road and entering his apartment complex. Mike stopped, lit up a cigarette and started working again, at his own pace it took another 10 minutes before he reached his building. He saw some civilians with shocked faces. The police downstairs tried to stop him and Mike showed up with his ID card.

"The door you broke upstairs, that apartment belongs to me, so I need to go up gentlemen." Mike said to the three offices downstairs as he kept walking towards the stairs.

Mike was about to keep his foot on the first stair on the staircase when he heard a loud screech of a car. He figured it was his colleagues', stopped and turned around and went back outside. Mike saw Matteo getting out of his car, who was visibly not in his best moods just by looking at his face.

"Really man, it's been less than forty eight hours since you came and you already had to make your mark didn't you?" Matteo asked Mike in a stern tone.

"Which part of be out of the spotlight did you not understand?" He added further.

"You speak as if I asked the Grim Reaper to collect his soul today." Mike shot back as both of them started walking towards the stairs.

Mike, can you please explain what Enzo was doing in your apartment" Matteo asked Mike.

"Helping us with the case." Mike responded as Matteo and himself were climbing up the stairs

"Mike, I am trying to help you here. It would be great if you could give me more detailed answers, just so your ex-father-in-law doesn't bite our asses tomorrow." Matteo said to Mike.

"Enzo met me at the hospital, he wanted to speak in private about what was happening and that's why he was in the apartment, now he's dead." Mike said to Matteo as they reached his apartment.

The door lay open as the authorities were inside collecting evidence, Enzo's body was on a stretcher. There were police stewarts almost everywhere inside the apartment; one of them was checking the bullet mark on the wall, another the broken windows, the half empty Scotch bottle and the used glasses. Even Mike's jacket which he left on the table two days ago was being checked.

"Well, I guess I'm not sleeping here tonight…uhhhhh Evidence." Mike said as he looked around.

"You should call your ex father-in-law, maybe he has a couch or you can call your ex, Mariella, that would be a lovely conversation in the current scenario." Matteo said sarcastically looking at Mike.

"Lovely idea!?" Mike looked at Matteo, his voice filled with contempt.

"Where the heck is Federico, let me call him." Matteo said to Mike, as if he just realised something.

"Don't worry about it, I sent them somewhere close by to check on some tire marks and to see if a specific vehicle could be tracked." Mike said to Matteo.

"What do you mean nearby, are you on to something?" Matteo asked Mike.

"I think, I located where the shots were fired from, found some tire marks on the road where the vehicle was most likely parked, the shot game from those two buildings about three hundred metres from here, we might need to review the CCTV footage from the area. By the time I reached there, when I called you earlier, the assassin got away, so our best bet is to find the vehicle, and see if we get clues from there. So I asked Federico to go to that location and check for further clues." Mike said to Matteo as he pointed towards the two buildings from the window.

"Captain Michelangelo Costa? Sir may we know what happened here?" One of the police officers on the scene asked Mike.

"Short version, Enzo came to threaten me back off this investigation and revenge, involving the murder of his boss Alessio, by the time he was done speaking, he got shot and died as you can see. Nothing else happened apart from him finishing some of my scotch. You can write that on your report." Mike responded to the officer.

"That is all?" The officer asked Mike again.

"Yeah, if I were you guys I would go to Alessio's warehouse and pretty much roundup everyone you can find in the property." Mike looked at the officer as he turned around and faced Matteo.

"Don't look at me, he got sniped at your house." Matteo said to Mike and he turned around.

While Matteo had finished saying this, Lorenzo and Federico stood at the entrance of the apartment. They got the attention of Mike, where Lorenzo asked him and Matteo to come outside to talk something in private. Mike and Matteo went outside the apartment and all four of them went downstairs towards the kids playing area away from all the police officers.

"So, I asked traffic control to check which vehicle went from the street towards the main road from the two buildings." Federico started to talk.

"And what did you find?" Matteo asked Federico.

"They say only two cars went from that street in a window of twenty minutes, so the one which matches the time frame where the shooting took place is a black Fiat Panda." Federico responded.

" Were they able to keep a track on where this car went?" Mike asked Federico.

"Not really, yeah apparently took multiple turns where there were no CCTV cameras so in theory he just disappeared in two minutes once he was out of that street." Federico said to Mike.

"And don't forget that this guy is actually driving something which is one of the most common cars out there, so he could be anywhere at this point." Lorenzo added on top of this.

"You're just telling that he disappeared." Matteo asked Lorenzo and Federico.

"That's what traffic control said to us although we have asked them to keep looking further, but as of now that seems to be the case, he's gone." Federico responded.

"Let the police write a report based on what Mike told them, as of now that's the story which is going out.

In the meantime, we keep digging from our original goal." Matteo said to Federico and the others.

"Mike, what did Enzo say? Did he give anything important at all?" Federico looked at Mike as he asked the question.

"Yeah, to keep it short, Enzo said he wouldn't even trust Claudio, that was pretty much the last thing he said before his brain ate a bullet." Mike responded to Federico.

"Can you be a bit more precise Mike, so we can actually think of our next move." Matteo said.

Mike started explaining whatever Enzo had said during their meeting at his house. Starting from their political ambitions, their plan to take over the entire mafia ring in Italy, how they were planning to fight against the Trentino family, the Albanian Mafia and all other details associated with that. Pretty much becoming the only kingmakers in the country.

"Claudio, freaking Claudio? Politicians cannot see this guy without an appointment, how the fuck are we supposed to get details out of him? Especially with the fourth murder happening in this chain, from whatever Enzo was supposed to have told you." Lorenzo exclaimed.

"Sometimes I used to wonder how you ended up in the Secret Service, and this is exactly why, drama queen." Mike said to Lorenzo.

"He's not exactly wrong you know, but yeah that was too much of an exaggeration." Matteo said, looking at both Mike and Lorenzo.

"Matteo, we kind of ignore the main point, we don't know who the next target is and Enzo is the third murder in less than a week. If Claudio is behind all of them as Enzo suspected, who is he even using? The mafia who is supporting him in Southern Italy or are we looking at new players now?" Federico asked Matteo.

"That is, if Claudio is indeed the culprit, what happens if he's in the hit list? We can't ignore that aspect, which seems more possible in the current scenario." Mike responded to Federico.

"Which way are we even taking this right now?" Lorenzo questioned everyone.

"I guess we're finally reaching the phase where we are forced to come out of the shadows a bit in this case." Matteo responded to Lorenzo.

"Do you think the boss can actually move some strings, where we might even be able to speak to this guy, without taking off a future minister probably?" Mike looked at Matteo as he lit up a cigarette.

"Let's decide this tomorrow. For now, Lorenzo and Federico, I want you guys to go to traffic control and see what you can find further. Myself and Mike, we're going to finish off whatever is left upstairs and let's all reconvene in the office tomorrow." Matteo said to everyone.

Federico and Lorenzo nodded their heads in acknowledgement, turned around and went towards their cars. Mike, on the other hand, continued smoking his cigarette as he started walking to the entrance leading towards the stairs of the apartment in the building. Matteo took his phone out and started texting something to Domenico, and he also started walking towards the stairs. Mike stopped a bit to throw down the cigarette as Matteo got up with them.

"Why in your apartment Mike? Couldn't you have had the meeting somewhere else?" Matteo questioned Mike.

"This is why." Mike reached into his pocket and handed over the note from Enzo to Matteo, which he got earlier in the day at the hospital.

"It was his gig, I could either play by his rules or not play at all. It's that simple, we've got something by playing it right, haven't we? If anything, it's my ass on fire and it's been on fire for too long that I don't even feel it anymore." Mike added as he started walking up the stairs.

"Do you have to take everything so personal Mike?" Matteo said to Mike, trying to get him to see his point of view.

"I didn't take it personally; I was just giving you my opinion. Sometimes it comes out in a not so friendly way, but it doesn't mean that it's not true." Mike replied as they reached the apartment again via the stairs.

Upon walking to the apartment, Mike noticed that Enzo's body was still inside the apartment and they hadn't taken it to the hospital, to follow departmental procedures. Mike got a bit irritated, and it didn't make things any better when he noticed two police officers checking the dining table and the wood it was made of. He flew into a mini rage rant.

"Jesus Christ! Is there a circus going on here, what are you waiting for, €5 per ticket to see Enzo's body opening for public view?" He asked in a high pitched tone smacking his head.

"You two over there, yeah that's rosewood, and I'll tell you exactly where I bought it as well, why don't you make yourself useful and try to take his body downstairs and to the hospital." Mike added further.

"Constable Gennaro right? Why don't you ask your Chief Assistant, who is standing downstairs to come up, please?" Matteo said to one of the constables.

"Yes, Sir." The Constable replied and he left the apartment quickly.

Mike and Matteo stood by while all the officers inside the apartment started to work at a frantic pace. Enzo's body was immediately taken downstairs, four or six of them were still collecting evidence from the apartment.

The chief assistant who had been summoned earlier, just came inside as Matteo turned around to see him.

“I think you would be more useful if you stayed here, please make sure that the entire place is cordoned off and you do some police work upstairs, huh?” Matteo said.

“I need some of your men to check those two buildings over there, ask everyone on the apartments facing my place here, whereabouts, alibi and empty places for the day, everything. Make sure it’s done, tonight, even if you have to wake the occupants.” Mike said to the Chief Assistant.

“Just be sure to drop the report off in our office, so we see it first thing in the morning.” Mike said to the chief assistant, while he and Matteo started going down, making their way to their respective cars.

5

Mentor

"Mike you can sleep at the guest bedroom." Matteo said as he got inside his car.

"It's no problem, I got it under control." Mike responded.

"I wasn't asking, just get your ass inside the car." Matteo said as he started the vehicle

"And he calls me stubborn and wonders where I got it from." Mike said as he went towards Matteo's car and got on the backseat.

"Since when did you start sitting in the back seat?" Matteo looked at Mike a bit surprised.

"Just wanted to lie down a bit, no other reason." Mike responded.

"Ok, make yourself comfortable, I guess." Matteo said as he started the car.

Mike said nothing all through the ride to Matteo's house, he was deep in thought all the while. Matteo noticed this, but he didn't say anything and left Mike to be on his own, while he focused on the road. They reached his house in about an hour with the traffic. He opened the gate and drove the car inside the house. Mike got down while Matteo was about to drive the car inside the garage and he went towards an orange tree in the garden, taking a fruit hanging there. He started peeling off its zest and eating it while Matteo parked the car and came towards the front door to open it, leaving the door open, he went inside. Mike walked slowly towards the house but he was more intent on finishing the fruit first. He went inside the house and noticed Matteo was setting up the table, with two plates.

"I have some leftover pasta which I made in the morning, that should be enough for the both of us." Matteo said to Mike.

"I'm not complaining, do you need any help?" Mike asked.

"Why don't you just heat the pasta from the fridge and bring it over here? What do you want to drink by the way? Coffee, juice or more alcohol?" Matteo asked Mike.

"Juice is good or even water." Mike responded as he went into the kitchen.

"What type of juice? Carrots, peach or apple?" Matteo asked again, as he was opening the mini fridge in the hallway near the TV.

"Apple is good." Mike responded while he was taking the pasta out of the fridge, putting it inside the microwave.

"Make sure you bring the ricotta cheese as well while you're coming." Matteo said to Mike.

"Seriously, I can understand why your wife went on vacation alone with your daughter." Mike said, taking the cheese from the fridge.

"I'll take that as a compliment." Matteo said while bringing a bottle of juice for Mike and some wine for himself.

Mike brought the pasta to the table and put it evenly on both plates and kept one plate at the chair, where Matteo kept the wine bottle on his side. Mike poured the juice in a glass, kept it on his side of the table, picked the plate from the table and started eating while he was standing. Matteo sat down and started eating and poured a glass of wine for himself.

"So what are you planning on telling Domenico about the case tomorrow?" Mike asked Matteo.

"What is there to ask? We need to find a way to talk to Claudio without triggering his suspicion, if indeed he was behind the murder of Alessio and Enzo." Matteo responded.

"The sticking point here is Vincenzo. One thing I don't understand is there was a clear pattern in terms of injury marks on the bodies of Vincenzo, Silvio and Alessio." Mike said to Matteo.

"And you're saying it could be someone else behind the death of Enzo?" Matteo asked Mike while taking a sip of wine.

"Maybe, I mean, I think he was the only one who was killed mercifully. Compared to him all the other three were pretty much straight-forward tortured to death. The killer made sure that they actually craved death, to stop being tortured further. I just can't shake the feeling that there are different people involved here not just one person again, maybe different gangs, I don't know, I just can't shake this feeling." Mike said to Enzo as he kept walking up and down between Matteo's chair and the end of the table which was easily twelve feet long.

"You got a point but Mike, let's stop talking about work and murders for a few minutes, maybe until we finish eating dinner." Matteo said to Mike and he continued eating.

"I was just keeping the conversation going, but sure." Mike responded while he pulled the chair and sat down at the table next to Matteo.

"Did you speak to Mariella? She did leave you a voice message before you came back from your supposedly first vacation right? You wanna talk about it?" Matteo said to Mike.

"What is there to talk about? We are both divorced for a reason, I think it's better that way." Mike responded to Matteo as he continued eating.

"I am not a mind reader, but she did play a part in you being back in the force, earlier than expected, so a simple acknowledgement to her on that would not be a bad idea." Matteo said to Mike.

"What's the point, nothing's going to change." Mike said as he ate.

"Mike, there are some things you need to let go, the death of your unborn son is not your fault. You being shot at wasn't your fault, you fighting with Mariella about issues in your marriage while gunshots were taken by Alessio's gang, wasn't your fault. You losing control over a car with a shattered window wasn't your fault. It's about time you stopped dwelling in self-pity, stopped blaming yourself. If anything, the ones responsible are already dead. I understand why you can't let this go. I have known you since your days in the orphanage and I know you better than anyone else around you. That's why I keep repeating this, you already lost your marriage, don't lose anything else which you might regret in a few years time." Matteo said and patted Mike on the shoulder.

"I know, or at least I think I know, but I hear you." Mike responded while nodding his head slowly.

"Then why didn't you call her? Dude, do you understand your marriage was falling apart before that incident broke it off completely? Despite all that, that woman still cares for you. Believe me, in this current world, that is a lot." Matteo said to Mike.

"I will Matteo, right after dinner, I promise! I don't think I've said it out loud too many times but I appreciate what you have done for me in the past twenty years and I still appreciate what you're doing for me even now." Mike said as he cleaned up his plate.

"It's fine, what can I say, you had potential. It's good to see my judgement on you since I saw you at the orphanage has not been proven wrong." Matteo said as he got up took his plate and moved to Mike's chair.

"So how much am I paying for the session the standard rate of €60 for one hour as my therapist?" Mike said with a big grin on his face.

"I have a better idea, you can do the dishes and I am going to bed." Matteo responded as he put his plate on top of Mike's empty plate.

"Definitely not the standard payment method I was expecting." Mike replied sarcastically as he started to clear the table.

"Just keep the volume down if you want to watch TV. Guest room or the couch, just sleep wherever you feel comfortable. Good night." Matteo said and walked upstairs to his bedroom.

"Good night, I'll see you in the morning." Mike said to Matteo as he went to the kitchen picking up the dishes from the dining table.

Mike went to the kitchen, put the dishes down on the kitchen table and saw the sink was almost full with dirty dishes. He facepalmed with a sigh as he said.

"I just had to open my mouth, I just had to make one sarcastic comment of course." Mike said to himself, as he opened the dishwasher.

Mike took out his phone, he opened Spotify and went to his favourites, he found the playlist of his favourite band, " Poets of The Fall" and started playing their songs and kept his phone on the kitchen table. Mike opened the dishwasher and started emptying the sink, for someone who wasn't a fan of housework, the music did seem to make him forget what he was doing, Mike singing the song along while filling up the dishwasher. By the time the second song had finished, he had finished putting the dishes inside the machine, he took a dishwashing capsule, stuck it inside the machine, turned the switch on and closed it. He started whistling as he took his phone from the table and went through his messages. He opened WhatsApp and scrolled through the last message Mariella had sent him. She had written earlier, asking if Mike was ok, it was fairly obvious she had heard the news of Enzo's death at his apartment. Mike started writing her a text, but changed his mind on the original wording he had typed in. He deleted whatever he had written earlier and wrote:

"Hey, am good, am ok and sorry I didn't text you earlier but I just wanted to say thank you for speaking to your dad again the other day." Writing this, Mike hit the send button.

No sooner had Mike sent the text, Mariella responded back within a couple of minutes and she had written a big text.

"Hey, good to hear from you and it's no problem. I heard what had happened since you joined the force. I knew you were busy with the case, and also knew what happened in your house in the evening, so it's good to hear that you are fine. I just hope you're ok emotionally as well. Where are you staying for the night? Let me know if you need my help?" She had texted.

"Hmmm, heard it from TV or from your dad? I'm doing ok, not going to lie, I had a bit of a roller coaster with not letting my personal emotions judge my professional side. I will admit though, it feels good to know the bastards who were responsible are dead and will be worm food. I am staying at Matteo's for the night. I think I might find a different place to stay for a week or so from tomorrow, if he lets me. Why are you awake at this time? It's almost 11PM. Aren't you working tomorrow morning?" Mike responded back.

"Saw the news on TV, justice had to prevail at some point, I know it's late, I was watching something on Netflix, lost track of time. I was actually about to go to sleep when I saw your text so I responded." Mariella texted back.

Mike started typing another text message, but before he sent it, he changed his mind again and deleted the text. He closed the app, clicked his tongue and made a call to Mariella. She picked up the phone after three rings.

"Hey, I know you said you are about to go to bed but do you think we can get a coffee sometime over the weekend, unless your boyfriend is having a problem, or even your dad or even you." Mike said to Mariella while mumbling through the words.

"Sure, I don't think anyone is going to have a problem with that, unless you cancel at the last minute." Mariella responded.

"I'll try not to. Saturday afternoon? That works, right?" Mike asked Mariella.

"Yeah, anywhere between noon till 3 or 4PM should be fine." She responded back.

"Great, I will see you then. Let me get back to you on Friday, to fix a spot." Mike said to Mariella.

"Sure, you go get some sleep as well, I think you need it after the past couple of days. Good Night." Mariella said.

" I will, anyways, get some sleep then and talk to you soon." Mike said to Mariella as he disconnected the phone.

"Well that's a start." Mike thought to himself and shoved his phone in his pocket.

Mike walked to the hall and sat on the couch. He was contemplating if he wanted to watch TV, he kept looking at the remote for a few seconds before deciding against it. Mike took a cigarette from his pack and lit it. Mike turned on his phone and went through his photo album, he scrolled through the pictures and opened the album which contained pictures of his old car in an accident. The next few pictures showed Mike bloodied in the head and hands, he had pictures of Mariella in a hospital bed.

He went through another set of pictures which showed newspaper articles of the car crash. The car overturned and on the side of the road crashed into a parked stationery semi truck. Mike put his head down on the couch and started to think about that day of the accident and the events which led to it.

Mike had first met Mariella at a party organised by her father. The conversation started because Mike had gotten drunk and ended up throwing up on her dress that night. Not the ideal way for an introduction. In the grand scheme of things, it didn't seem to matter as they both grew fond of each other after Mike had called her the next day to apologise and one thing led to another, it wasn't long before they started dating and officially becoming a couple within a few weeks. Within four months they had already moved in and within seven months of meeting each other, they were already married.

The relationship had moved fast but that didn't seem to bother them. Issues in their marriage eventually started with Mike, simply being himself. In short, Mike had a problem. Family life after being a loner for years. It was all fun and games when he was just dating but marriage and new responsibilities was something hard for him to adjust. Mike just didn't know how to split between family life and his professional life. This had brought multiple misunderstandings before verbal fights became all too common between the couple. Things only got even worse when Mike picked up the investigation headed by Matteo, to investigate the big names in the Italian crime ring from politicians, to influential businessmen. Under the watch of his ex father-in-law Domenico, who didn't want him on the case and preferred Mike, worked on his marriage. Mike on the other hand though, didn't back off and Matteo had also wanted Mike to be a part of this team. In a clash between professional and personal life, Mike chose professional. The case was complicated, and the fact that it was a secret investigation, meaning that Mike was away from the house even longer didn't help either.

Mike also started getting on the bad side of almost all the major gangs and their bosses, especially Alessio, whose last three shipments of drugs were busted by Mike, which ended up costing Alessio well over forty million Euros. In the meantime, at home, Mariella had become pregnant. Rather than bringing peace between the couple, it became more stressful as Mike was not around when Mariella needed him, effectively almost being a single parent even if she was married. They had a doctor's appointment one day, unfortunately Mike was late to pick her up. On their way to the hospital, Mariella was upset with Mike and was making her feelings known. Mike, also not backing down, was speaking from his perspective when gunshots were heard and two bullets came through the glass, one bullet hitting Mike's shoulder while shattering the driver's glass. Mike lost control of the car as it overturned, crashing into a parked semi truck. The impact knocked both of them into unconsciousness. The next thing Mike remembered was being in hospital with a broken wrist and a couple of cracked ribs and some facial injuries. The worst part was reserved for his partner, Mariella, who had lost the baby.

Mike went into a shell blaming himself for what had happened, going into depression and in general, ruining whatever strings the marriage was lasting on. Mike never got over his guilt and had applied for divorce, he blamed himself for ruining Mariella's life and felt she would be better off without him. Even if people and Mariella herself tried to change his mind, Mike never really got over the guilt and the blame he put on himself for the loss of his unborn son. Alessio, who had ordered the hit on Mike that day, could not be brought to justice. Mike blamed himself again, starting to question his professional career even. Becoming more erratic and with vengeance on his mind, Mike had become more and more distant with all his close people. This only gave credence, in his view, to end the marriage because Mike was not the same person he was.

It's been almost a year since Mike and Mariella had divorced, against the advice of his closest friends, which included only three people he normally trusted in his life: Federico, Lorenzo and his mentor Matteo. He barely took any time off to fix his personal life. Mike chose to dive deeper into the rabbit hole, instead; he was hooked on the chase, a burning desire to bring down the empires of the people in the case they were dealing in. He had a special place reserved for Alessio, but he wanted to bring down everyone who was associated with him.

The Marchesis and the Trentinos, the two biggest gangs in almost all organised crime in Southern and Central Italy, their connections to the Italian mafia and also the Albanian and Russian mafia has always been a big problem for law enforcement. Their connections ran deep into every line enforcement agency, they had people on their payroll in every department possible. Any slight hint of an investigation on them before even the team was selected, they would be tipped off. To make matters worse, both gangs had one prominent member in the Parliament with politicians backing them up and turning a blind eye to their activities. The ongoing investigation took about a year for Matteo to even find whom he could trust to lead this investigation on. Mike was the wildcard, unorthodox and highly effective, who never cared about the rules and only cared about the results. Mike's next target, Claudio Marchesi, continued his family's legacy in organised crime. Vincenzo's younger brother, specialising in arms and narcotics trafficking, building a reputation as a ruthless negotiator, eliminating all competition, killings held regularly as a statement of power. A man so feared that politicians in certain counties had to get his permission to implement a government policy. Claudio was famous for making people disappear, especially the ones who have got under his skin, exposing some of his dark secrets. The list included journalists, bloggers, police officers and rivals. There was a very good possibility, the current series of murders were linked to Claudio somehow, but there was no way to establish it yet.

"One heck of a memory. I should write a goddamn book about this" Mike said to himself as he continued smoking while thinking about the past events until present day.

Mike got up from the couch and went outside and took a small walk in the garden. He looked at the sky and saw the moon was reaching its full moon phase. He checked the time on his watch and it was well over midnight. Mike went to the orange tree, got himself another fruit and started to peel the zest off while eating it. He saw the lights in Matteo's room was already out and he assumed that he was asleep.

"Hard to imagine a week ago I was thinking about where to go on vacation. Life!." He exclaimed while going back into the house.

6

Suspects and Disagreements

Mike finished the last orange piece and went to the bathroom, washed his hands, splashed water over his face and walked to the guest bedroom. He got on top of the bed, pulled the blanket over, checked the alarm settings on his phone and turned the aeroplane mode on and put the phone on the lamp stand. He turned off the lights as he fell asleep, after saying a short prayer.

"Good morning sunshine, you better take a shower and get ready soon, the chief and the team will soon arrive." Matteo woke up Mike as he said this.

"Uhhh, here, ehhh? What time is it, how long was I asleep?" Mike asked Matteo as he was still trying to come to his senses.

"It's 7AM. you didn't oversleep; it's just that everyone will be here by 9." Matteo said.

"Everyone? Who is everyone? Define everyone, you just kick me out of bed and started speaking, people are still disoriented here." Mike said to Matteo, yawning loudly.

"As I said earlier, the chief and the team are coming to my house. You see this house you're actually staying in currently? This house, get your ass up and tidy yourself." Matteo said to Mike.

"I should have got one of those IT jobs where I have to start working only at noon or something." Mike said as he got out of bed.

"It's still possible, just help finishing this operation before that." Matteo said to Mike as he handed him a cup of coffee.

"Yeah, thanks for the career advice." Mike responded and he started sipping coffee.

Matteo just turned around and walked away without saying anything. Mike started walking to the hall, finishing his coffee by then and put the mug on the dining table. He headed towards the bathroom, closing the door. He jumped into the shower and in his own typical fashion, took a long one. He came back out and got dressed and went into the kitchen. Matteo was upstairs freshening up; in the meantime, Mike took a loaf of bread from the kitchen cupboards, took some cheese and vegetables from the fridge and started making a sandwich, for both him and Matteo. He put the sandwiches on a plate and went to the dining table in the hall, keeping one plate for Matteo. He took the other plate to the table before the TV. He turned the TV on and played an episode of Seinfeld from Netflix.

After the episode started, Mike put his feet on the table, got the plate on his lap and started eating the sandwich.

Matteo came downstairs on the completion of one of the episodes of the series, he went to the table and saw the sandwich Mike had made for him. He pulled a chair and started eating as he watched Mike watching TV with a half eaten sandwich in his hand.

"Would you mind keeping your foot off the table?" Matteo asked.

"Ohh sorry, I didn't notice you were down already." Mike responded to Matteo, taking his eyes off the TV.

"You don't need to wait for me to keep your foot down, finish your sandwich man, Jesus! You start watching TV and you completely forget where you are? How old are you, ten?!?" He said with irritation in his voice,

"I thought your bad mood was going to be reserved for when everyone is here, maybe you need one more coffee?" Mike responded as he continued eating the sandwich.

"You're not the only one who hates mornings." Matteo replied back to Mike.

Matteo had barely finished eating when his phone started to ring, and it was Lorenzo on the call. They had arrived a bit earlier with about fifteen minutes, and the entire team reached Matteo's house in an SUV. Matteo let the team inside while Mike was still sitting on the couch watching TV and finishing his sandwich. Everyone had arrived, even Mario, who had been recently out of Italy, enjoying his honeymoon and had just returned the previous night. Mario was asked first thing to join up for the meeting at Matteo's house. Everyone entered the house and Mario went straight to Mike.

"Good to see you again, Sir." Mario said to Mike.

"You too, Mario, I hope Bali was good." Mike asked Mario.

"It was, it was." Mario replied.

Before the conversation could continue any further, Domenico intervened and asked everyone to sit at the dining table. Everyone pulled a chair and sat at the table as Domenico looked straight at Mike.

"Mike, I am not going to roast you on this because Matteo already briefed me on whatever happened. The police also submitted their report before we came here, but dammit will you stop putting attention to this group and not blow this investigation." Domenico looked at Mike and said.

"It's not as if I wanted it, but as I said to Matteo, I could either play by Enzo's rule or not at all. Either way, we're going to need access to Claudio; the important question is, how the hell did the assassin know Enzo would be coming to my house? He had slipped a note to my collar, it was supposed to be a secret meeting, yet

I have his brain splattered all over my wall?" Mike asked, looking at everyone at the table.

"Do you feel it is an inside job?" Federico asked Mike.

'Either that or I tipped off the assassin, it just keeps getting mental the more I think about it, the four guys Enzo came to the hospital with, are they under surveillance? Mike asked Federico.

"Yeah, the police are keeping tabs and I asked them to round them up, we should get the information when they are locked up." Federico said to Mike.

"We need to speak to Claudio, Chief, I need this." Mike said to Domenico.

"No, we don't have access to Claudio, Mike. Not as a group at least." Domenico responded to Mike.

"On one hand, he could be the reason for three murders, on the other hand he could be the next target, either way there's no way to find a clear pattern without speaking to the guy who has the spotlight on him." Matteo said to the group.

"Apart from Claudio, who do you think the next target could be? If we assume Claudio is a target, there has to be a list which our assassin has made up." Domenico questioned Mike.

"Can you establish a link apart from Claudio who might be on this list, if the murders are actually following a specific matter? Maybe we can try and trace it all back to a major event in the past? Where a specific group of people were involved, and maybe we can link whoever was murdered now to that list and and we could go from there." Matteo looked at Mike and added further questions.

"I think I can answer that. I was going through our files on whatever we had collected in the past two years ever since this whole thing began." Mario said to the group.

"I could think of two specific cases where Claudio was involved which had the highest heat, this directly struck a nerve with Trentino and the Albanian mafia." He added further.

"Is this the murder of Joseph in regards to the five hundred kilos of cocaine shipment involved? is that one of the reasons you're talking about?" Lorenzo masked Mario.

"Yeah that is one of them, the next is supporting the crackdown on the Sicilian Mafia, which led to the murder of Antonino. One of the major reasons Trentino was able to win the elections was because he was endorsed by Antonino. This put Claudio in direct conflict with the Sicilian Mafia, the Albanian mafia and also with Trentino. Since Claudio did this for Vincenzo, who's political standing increased based on that crackdown, with the disguise of police involvement and the subsequent crime it brought down in those territories, we could safely assume that someone from that circle took out Vincenzo in the first place and they are going for Claudio next, these are the only two solid scenarios which give credentials for the ongoing chaos, the others, though big, don't really match our current issue." Mike said to the group before Mario could say anything.

"We need a warrant on Claudio, we need to pin them on something." Federico said to the group while drinking some water.

"Listen, I understand this will hit the news, if Claudio is indeed behind the latest murders, especially with his current political ambitions. But unless he speaks to us or we speak to him, I don't see the end of it. This guy is genuinely out for blood and he pulls another stunt like he did with the Sicilian Mafia, we're looking at this guy winning the election using the police as a proxy and literally turning Central and Southern Italy into a war zone." Mike said as he stood up.

"This operation was started to take down organised crime, Claudio will do it on his own terms, and the resulting fallout will actually bring even bigger chaos where he is in control of that chaos, that's scenario one. The next, our assassin takes out Claudio and a vacuum is created, small players fight between themselves to take his throne, which again is not good for Southern Italy at this point, we're fucked either way and the only thing we need to decide is which one is better." Mike added further as he looked at Domenico.

Domenico got up from his chair, reached into his pockets and got a cigarette pack, he lit one up and started walking back and forth for a couple of minutes. Everyone at the table just kept looking at him, he seemed to be deep in thought. Matteo looked at Mike and tilted his head towards Domenico, Mike got up from his chair and started walking towards Domenico, who stood at the entrance of the house, near the door with Matteo following Mike.

"Let me talk to someone, the death of Enzo, let's assume that Claudio is the next target and try to talk to him that way. This will most likely create news as people try to establish the link and the press will have a field day, as they dig up past stories from their side. this is the only way we can proceed, I believe." Domenico said to Mike and Matteo who stood nearby.

"We understand. We will wait for your further instructions." Matteo replied.

"I'll work with the boys and and see how we can proceed with this from our side." Mike responded from his end.

"Mike, why don't you start with the police report and and go from there, you guys can go upstairs if you need your space." Matteo said to Mike and he looked at the group sitting at the table.

"I think it's better we get going in that sense, I will try to dig further into the incidents which happened yesterday. Send it to the guys, I've already read the police report; I will get the debriefing from them and we will take it from there and we will wait for further instructions from you or the Chief." Mike said to Matteo as he asked his colleagues at the table to join him.

Mario, Lorenzo and Federico got up from the table and started walking outside, giving their salutes to Domenico as they left.

"So what did you geniuses find in the police report, were any of the tenants in the building see or hear something unusual? Anyone on the suspect list?" Mike asked while walking towards the SUV.

"The shot came through from the building on the left, one out of the two which you wanted to be checked, the assassin, he's definitely male, because he ended up tying both the owners, dumped them in the bedroom and took his shot. From what the owners told the police, the assassin was there for close to two hours." Federico said to Mike.

"Where are the owners currently? Are they still in the apartment?" Mike asked Federico.

"Yeah they were told not to go out of the city and inform us if they need to, one the local police to keeping tabs on the building and owners, they are currently in their apartment." Federico said to Mike.

"Let's get in the car and talk on the way." Mike said to the group.

Mike and his colleagues got into the car and drove out of Matteo's house, Federico was driving the car with Mike on the front seat next to the driver with Lorenzo and Mario at the back.

"Did you find anything useful at the traffic controller yesterday? Was there a remote possibility they could find this car?" Mike asked the group.

"Nothing useful, he made a clean getaway, it seemed like he had planned the whole thing to a dot." Lorenzo said to Mike.

"I still don't get it, how did the assassin know Enzo was going to be at my apartment? He came fully prepared, broke into the house on the opposite streets, got Enzo in one shot, and made a clean break and vanished. Mike said to Lorenzo as he turned around.

"Feels like an inside job, right?" Mario pitched in.

"Definitely an inside job, then again, I still don't understand how the assassin knew Enzo was going to be at my house? The four guys at the hospital or Enzo was bugged secretly and someone was listening to his conversation?" Mike looked around the car and said to his colleagues.

"Your guess is as good as ours Mike." Lorenzo said to Mike.

"By the way, where are you driving to? I thought we were going to the apartment building to interrogate the couple." Mike looked at Federico who was driving.

" Sorry, I thought we were going to the precinct. Let me take a left at the next street." Federico said, and he put on the car indicator and took a left.

"You're getting old Alfred Pennyworth, concentrate." Mike said, looking at Federico as Lorenzo and Mario burst into laughter.

"Hey Federico, answer me this, if you die on your Tombstone, are we writing, Alfred Pennyworth or Federico Biraghi?" Lorenzo asked Federico as he continued laughing.

"The important question here is, does your girlfriend know you as Federico or Alfred? Does she even know that you have a secret Life?" Mario added further as everyone in the car started laughing even more as Federico was driving looking indifferent to the comments.

"Come on guys, you need to come up with a new name or something, I'm getting used to it by now." Federico said as he continued driving.

"Ok Happy Hogan." Mike said while he looked at Federico, Mario and Lorenzo continued laughing further while Federico gave an irritated look at Mike.

"Why are you looking at me, you wanted a new name, you love Iron Man so I'm calling you Happy Hogan, if anything, it's wish granted." Mike added further as he took his phone and started looking at it so he didn't have to face Federico further, while continuing to laugh.

Federico drove for another ten minutes before they reached the Apartment Complex where the assassin had taken the shot from. Mike got down, along with Lorenzo and Mario while Federico drove to find a parking spot for the SUV. Mike found the police car, which was keeping watch of the building and when to talk to the cop, sitting inside the car.

"Good morning, Michelangelo Costa, AISI, anything suspicious or anyone looking suspicious ever since you came here?" Mike asked the policeman.

"Nothing of note sir." The policeman replied.

"The couple in whose apartment the assassin took the hit from, are they still upstairs?" Mike asked the policeman.

"Yes, that's their car which is parked over there, they have locked themselves in in ever since yesterday, the only time they open the door and spoke to someone, was to the police." the policeman responded.

"We will take it from here, thank you." Mike replied as he turned around and started walking towards Lorenzo and Mario, Federico in the meantime had also parked the car and came towards them.

"So what did he say?" Mario asked Mike.

"They are still upstairs, apparently they haven't spoken to anyone apart from the police since yesterday. I think I'll go upstairs alone, I don't want them to get the feeling that they are being harassed for something which is not even their fault, unless proven otherwise after the investigation." Mike said to the group.

"Ok, it makes sense." Federico replied agreeing with Mike.

"I am out of cigarettes anyway, I'm going to go to the tobacco shop then." Lorenzo responded.

"Can you do me a favour Federico?" Mike asked.

"What is it?" Federico asked Mike, who threw his car keys at him.

"Can you just bring my car here while I finish upstairs, I love you buddy." Mike said as he turned around and started walking towards the building.

"Jerk." Federico said as he turned around and started walking towards Mike's building, leaving Lorenzo and Mario controlling the laughter until Federico had moved a bit further.

Mike went inside the building and went towards the elevator. He pushed the button and saw that it was on the top floor, the elevator seemed to stop at every floor as Mike waited patiently. Finally it came to the ground floor, and an elderly couple with walking sticks stepped out. Mike smiled at them and waited until all left the elevator at their own pace. He went inside and pressed the button for the third floor, making his way to the apartment. He rang the doorbell and a voice from inside responded.

"Who is it?" It was a male voice from inside.

"Michelangelo Costa from AISI, Italian Secret Service, I just want to talk to you about yesterday, just a routine formality, nothing major." Mike said.

The man opened the door partially as he saw Mike's ID card which he flashed. Once he read the ID card, the man opened the door fully and let Mike in. Mike went inside the apartment; the man offered him to take a seat on one of the couches. His wife came outside from the other room, to see who it was.

"What do you want to know, Officer, we already told everything whatever happened yesterday to the other policemen." The man said.

"I understand that, I forgot to get your name and your wife's, sorry." Mike said to the man.

"Alessandro and that's my wife, Rebecca." The man replied.

"Please take a seat as well, you too Ma'am." Mike said to both of them.

"Like you said Alessandro, I did read the report on whatever you had said yesterday, I just wanted to understand a couple of things. Just for clarity's sake. So this guy had tied up both you and your wife for close to two hours, before you heard a slight gunshot and the door immediately closing within a few seconds, am I right?" Mike asked Alessandro.

"Yes, that is correct." Alessandro replied.

"He came as a food delivery agent, didn't he?" Mike asked again.

"Yes, we didn't order anything, he rang the doorbell and asked for my name. I opened the door just because he said the order came from here directly, he barged in through the door, pushing me inside. Then he held a gun to my face, told me and my wife to shut up and he forced me to tie her up first before he tied me up. He put a plaster over our mouths and made us walk at gunpoint into the bedroom. He made us lie down on the bed and tied both of our feets together. After that was done, he said he will be gone soon and him leaving us alive or dead, depended on how we were acting until he leaves, before he closed the door." Alessandro said to Mike nervously.

"And this man was about one hundred and eighty cms tall, had a deep voice and was wearing sunglasses and a helmet, so you could not see his face clearly, am I right Alessandro and Rebecca?" Mike asked the couple.

"Yes." Rebecca replied.

"May I know how both of you got untied again?" Mike asked the couple.

"Before leaving he had just shut the door without locking it, we heard a few knocks on the door before the police came inside noticing the door was open. They then came to the bedroom and saw both of us tied up. They were the ones who untied us, before asking what had happened and getting our statement and checking the apartment from head to toe and asking us not to leave town without getting any approvals from their side. They also mentioned that they might reach us in the future for any clarifications and for further investigation. Just like they had mentioned, you are here today." Alessandro replied to Mike.

"Mr. Michelangelo, officer, we're telling the truth, we do not know who this guy is, unfortunately he just used our apartment for whatever he did last evening. We just want to be left alone." Rebecca said to Mike.

"You will be, sorry to bother you. Take care of yourselves." Mike said to the couple as he stood up, walked to the door and let himself out.

Mike made his way to the elevator, he found it was right there on the third floor, it seemed no one had used it ever since he came to this floor. He got inside, pressed the button for the ground floor and made his way outside the building where his team were waiting for him.

"You found anything which could be useful." Federico asked Mike.

"Not really, they pretty much stuck to the same story which they had told the police yesterday. The assassin is smart, that's for sure." Mike responded to Federico.

Mike's phone started to ring while he was speaking, he checked who it was and noticed it was Matteo. He picked up the phone and said hello.

"Mike, the impossible happened, Claudio has agreed to meet but he only wants to speak to one member in the team and he wants it in a location of his choice." Matteo said over the phone.

"That is an interesting turn of events, did he give a location?" Mike asked Matteo.

"Not yet, we're just waiting to hear from him for now." Matteo said to Mike.

"Ok, we wait." Mike responded as he disconnected the call.

Just as he took the phone away from his ear, Mario shot a question right away.

"Did we hear it right? Claudio agreed for a meeting?" He asked Mike.

"Apparently yes." Mike responded and shook his head.

"Which brings us to a scenario where he is afraid? I mean if he was behind Enzo's murder, why would he want to see us?" Lorenzo asked the team.

"Or he figured Domenico is reaching out, figured there is heat on him and is calling to tell us to fuck off, so we keep our heads on our body." Mike responded.

"You think that could be the case?" Mario asked Mike.

"Well the chief said we would know later in the day where we are supposed to meet him, let's find out." Mike replied to the team looking at them.

"Hey Mike, the four stooges from the hospital are in police custody, just got the notification." Federico said to Mike.

"Let's go, I need to speak to these assholes." Mike said with Federico throwing him his car keys.

Mike got into his car and the others got into the SUV and started driving towards the police station. This was the first time Mike was driving his car after the breakdown two days ago. He felt the car was much smoother, it seemed like his mechanic had done a lot more work than just fixing the reason for the breakdown the other night. Mike turned on some music, looked in the rear view mirror and saw his steam right behind him. They weaved through the streets of Naples and reached the police station in about twenty minutes. Mike parked the car, got down and went to his colleagues who were getting out of the SUV themselves; a minute later Mike reached the police station.

"Can I borrow a lighter, mine's out of juice?" Mike asked his team.

"Here, use mine." Lorenzo gave his lighter to Mike, who proceeded to start lighting up a cigarette.

The team went into the police station and met the officer in charge and introduced themselves.

"Michelangelo Costa, AISI, believe you have been expecting us. Those are my colleagues Federico, Mario and Lorenzo. Can we see the four accused you have rounded up?" Mike asked the officer, who asked them to follow him to the holding cell where all the men, who were with Enzo at the hospital, were held.

"Where did you pick these guys up by the way?" Mike asked the Officer.

"From a stripclub, two of them high on cocaine, one of them passed out drunk and another having manic sex in a drug fuelled session." The Officer said as they reached the holding cell, opening the door for Mike and his colleagues.

"Hello ladies, I think we already met yesterday, while Enzo was still alive and talking with me in the hospital, we have suspicion that all the four of you or at least one of you is working with the murderer, I don't believe a lot of people knew Enzo was meeting me in the evening, so the four of you have anything to say? Something useful for once in your lives would be nice." Mike said to them the moment he entered the room.

The four members from Enzo's gang were seated together round the table, Mike and his colleagues surrounded the table, each of them standing right behind each accused.

"Believe you were asked a question Fabio, are you going to answer or any of your colleagues supposed to do it?" Mario asked Fabio, keeping his hands on his shoulders and applying pressure on Fabio's collarbone.

"So how does the election process happen in a gang? Alessio is gone and now Enzo, so there is no leader in your universe, so do you guys follow an election process or something like regular people? Or it depends on how many people each killed or is there some sort of drinking game? How does it work?" Lorenzo asked the group.

"Is this the reason why you idiots were celebrating last night? Knowing Enzo was going to be taken out of the equation? I mean seriously, drugs, booze, girls, you guys had the full package last night and still were before you got picked up in the morning. So what's the reason you four assclowns were celebrating like there was no tomorrow last night? You four being silent is really not going to help anyone, by the time your lawyers actually show up, missing a few teeth and a few broken ribs might be the least painful activity you guys face today." Mike said to the four accused.

"Fabio, Sandro, Gerardo, Pietro, it's quite a record you guys have here, so tell us, why did you snitch on Enzo? Who did you snitch to? Why was the person keeping tabs on Enzo? How much were you paid for it?" Federico questioned the four accused.

All the four of them were still dazed by the effects of the drugs and the alcohol by the looks on their faces, but it also smacked of confusion. Mike was noticing all of this while the questions were being asked.

"If someone doesn't start speaking in the next ten seconds, It's not going to end well for one of you." Mike said to the group, sounding angry in his tone.

"We were celebrating my birthday, the celebrations kept continuing till the morning and we didn't know about Enzo's murder until the police barged to our private party and dragged us here." Fabio responded to the question.

"Ok, you still did not answer the main question, why were you all snitching on Enzo and who are you snitching to? Claudio or someone in the same circles? I need answers and I don't care how you get them." Mike said to Fabio.

"It doesn't matter how much you rage at us, we had nothing to do with what happened last evening." Fabio responded to Mike's question.

"And we're supposed to believe that?" Mike said to Fabio.

"Yeah, no option other than believe what I tell you. Maybe you should start taking care of people under your watch Mike, seems like anyone who comes under your protection, ends up dying, just like in the past even if they are not even born yet." Fabio said to Mike with a grin.

Mike calmly looked at Fabio and gave him a smile as Fabio looked at him still having the sarcastic grin.

"Did it ever occur to you why your lawyers haven't shown up yet?" Mike asked as Fabio's smile went away.

"No one even knows you four were picked off the streets. With all the murders happening, I don't think anyone would think anything odd if four more bodies showed up randomly somewhere in the streets of Naples. There's easier ways to kill yourself then get on our nerves in the current scenario, since I feel you need a practical demonstration, this is what I mean." Mike punched Fabio right in the nose breaking it and blood started pouring out of his nose.

"So how about you three? Still feeling cocky or do you need any practical lessons from my side further?" Mike added while looking at the others.

"Listen Mike, we really do not know, right after Enzo left the hospital he said he had some unfinished business and told us to leave him alone." Sandro said to Mike.

"What time did this happen?" Mike asked Sandro while moving to his chair.

"A few minutes after you two finished talking and when we left the hospital around 3PM.?" Sandro responded.

"Did he mention anything at all where he was going or what he was about to do?" Mike asked Sandro.

" No, he just got into his car and left and told us to have a fun night." Sandro replied to Mike.

"Listen man, I know that's not the answer you're looking for but that is exactly what happened, you gotta believe us here, we're not working for anyone else and we didn't definitely betray Enzo." Pietro said from his side.

"Did Enzo and Alessio mention anything about Claudio in the past month specifically?" Mike asked Pietro.

"Yes, they were feeling Claudio was going overboard in trying to find out who murdered Vincenzo and this was affecting their operations, because Claudio was putting his political ambitions before anything else until the elections were over." Pietro said to Mike as Fabio was still in pain.

"Anything further apart from that?" Mike asked Pietro, still not looking very convinced.

"Nothing as far as we know. Listen, we have the Trentino's and the mafia to worry about, so as much as it's frustrating to go through with Claudio's decisions right now, we just made peace with it. Actually, why get in the bad books of Claudio and get ourselves burnt from every side possible? This was the same feeling of Alessio and Enzo, even if they were frustrated to the core." Pietro responded to Mike's question.

Mike turned around and went out of the room after he heard Pietro answer his last question, his colleagues followed suit and all of them met outside the room.

"They're just telling the same thing which we figured, namely, Enzo and Alessio were both frustrated with Claudio but we still don't have any solid evidence to think Claudio pulled off yesterday's events, we are still in a dead end about who snitched on Enzo, that the murderer was waiting at that apartment building for Enzo to show up at my house and pulled off the hit." Mike was speaking to his colleagues and as he was about to continue further, Federico received a phone call which he attended.

"Federico, could you pass on the phone to Mike." Matteo said on the other line.

"Mike it's for you." Federico said as he threw his phone to Mike who got it.

"Hey, why didn't you just call my number if you want to talk to me?" Mike asked Matteo over the phone.

"Because your phone was not reachable, it's that simple. Anyways we have news about Claudius meeting tomorrow, he only wants to meet one of us as mentioned, so do you want to go?" Matteo asked Mike.

"Sure I will go, when and what time are we doing this?" Mike asked Matteo.

“He is apparently going to visit Vincenzo’s grave at 10AM in the morning, you have a window of thirty minutes to talk to him.” Matteo said to Mike.

“Am I expecting company?” Mike asked.

“His usual bodyguards, try not to get shot in a cemetery.” Matteo said to Mike.

“I will try my best not to. By the way, it’s at a dead end with the four guys who accompanied Enzo to the hospital. Their story seems consistent and based on their body language, they are telling the truth. Enzo being snitched is something else, maybe his phone is hacked and someone is listening and watching him through his phone activity. I guess, we keep looking through their gang and let me see if I can ruffle any feathers with Claudio tomorrow.” Mike said to Matteo.

“Ok, I will inform the Chief about it and let me see what the cyber crime department have found based on Enzo’s phone.” Matteo said to Mike.

“Thanks, actually, we’ll check from our side with the cyber security, i just need your help in finding Claudio’s schedule for tomorrow, before and after our meeting window, if you can.” Mike said to Matteo.

“I will see what I can find.” Matteo said to Mike.

“Thanks, I’ll see you later.” Mike responded to Matteo and disconnected the call.

Mike started rubbing his forehead for a few seconds, thinking hard, he looked at Federico and threw his phone back to him. He then looked at Lorenzo and Mario and spoke to all of them in general.

"I think we are done here boys, these guys aren't going to give us shit." Mike said to his team.

"So we check Enzo's phone with cybersecurity? That's your next step." Lorenzo asked Mike, trying to reconfirm the plan.

"Yeah and we need to search for bugs in his car and also his house, they were tracking him somehow and we just need to know how, so now Mario and Lorenzo, could you guys initiate a second search on Enzo's house and check it for bugs? Federico, can you go to cybersecurity and find out the details on his phone and also initiate a bug search on Enzo's car. He's definitely being tapped and we need to know from where, after that we can find out who." Mike said to the team.

"We're on it." Lorenzo said to Mike.

"What are you going to do?" Federico asked Mike.

"I have some personal business with my ex-wife, and I think I need some closure. I owe it to her too, before I meet Claudio tomorrow. Just give me the file though." Mike responded to Federico.

"Good luck buddy." Federico said to Mike, he gave him a hug, gave the file he held to Mike and left with Lorenzo and Mario following him.

Mike waited and saw all of them leave the police station while he was walking behind them. He then turned around and walked over to the police chief and began to talk about the four arrested members from Enzo's gang who were held at the station.

"One of them, Fabio, has a broken nose and would need medical assistance; you can give them access to their lawyers but before that, book them on all the charges which are in this file. Also, add that they were caught with drugs when you arrested them and add it on top of this list. Would be nice to have less idiots off the streets for a while." Mike said to the police chief.

"How do I explain the broken nose?" He asked Mike, trying to imply he was the boss in his station.

"Resisting arrest and you had to use force, will it do? So difficult to file a fake incident, don't act like you've never broken protocol before. Thank you for your help; we will be in touch." Mike said as he gave a smile and walked out of the police station, without caring what anyone at the station thought.

7

CLOSURE AND A BEGINNING

Mike kept walking to his car and took his mobile phone out. He went through his contact list and searched for Mariella and made a call to her. The phone kept ringing until it went to voicemail, Mike disconnected the call and put the phone in his pocket and got into his car. He put the keys in and started the car when his phone began to ring, he checked who it was. It was Mariella. He answered the phone and she began to speak immediately as the line connected.

"Hey, is everything ok? Are you alright?" Mariella asked Mike.

"Yeah everything is fine, come on, we just spoke last night. Only, the case is a pain in the ass but everything else is fine." Mike responded.

"Ok, I thought that something was wrong since you called out of the blue." She said to Mike, sounding relieved.

"No nothing's wrong, sorry wasn't meant to cause panic. I just sent the guys to check some details regarding the case and I have some free time. I know, I asked to meet you on Saturday, but if you are free now, can we meet today? Just thought it would be nice to see you." Mike said to Mariella.

"I am working from home today, and I should be done maybe in an hour." Mariella responded.

"How about lunch? Around 1PM. maybe?" He asked.

"Yeah that should work, do you have a place in mind?" Mariella asked Mike.

"How about La Masardona? It"s been a while since I've been there, it's close to you; I could get a pizza and you can order something else if you want or we could both share a pizza."

"It should be fine; we will think about the food when I am there. I'll see you at 1PM. then." Mariella responded.

"1PM. it is, I'll see you there." Mike said.

"See you Mike." Mariella responded as she disconnected the call from her side.

Mike saw the phone as it went to the homescreen and threw it on the seat next to him. He started the car and drove towards the restaurant even though he had well over an hour to kill. Mike drove through the streets of Naples and reached the restaurant in about twenty minutes. He went inside and ordered a coffee and he came out for a smoke while the coffee was being made and kept eyes on the TV with the news playing on. The news showed an event which featured some high-profile individuals who were attending an opera in the city. Filippo Patrizi, the billionaire socialite, a man with Anisomelia, who was known for his NGOs works towards the homeless and disabled. Gerardo Lucchi, CEO of the Lucchi industries around Europe were on the forefront of the videos. Mike kept watching the news and continued smoking as he noticed his coffee was being brought to the table. He finished the smoke and went inside, took his phone out, put on his headphones and started playing an online video game while drinking his coffee and eating a croissant. Minutes passed by and he was interrupted by his headphones rudely removed from his ears from behind. Mike turned to find Mariella standing behind him smiling and rolling her eyes when she saw him playing a video game on his phone.

"Didn't you complete this game about a year ago?" Mariella asked as she put Mike's headphones on the table and went to the opposite chair on the table.

"Well not on this difficulty, there is only so much TV series and music I can listen to and I got bored of watching a bunch of billionaires attending the Opera as the flash news in the city." Mike said as he took his headphones and put them inside his jacket pocket.

"Are you irritated because your face is not on the TV?" Mariella joked.

"I don't think I'm too photogenic, and you know me: I hate to be on the public eye, that's why I'm on the Secret Service, I don't even exist on most police cases." Mike responded as he bit down on his croissant.

"The problem with you is you disappeared even from your private life. Isn't that the main issue?" Mariella responded, and her smile disappeared a bit.

"I know, that's why I wanted to see you." Mike responded as he asked for the waitress to come over to the table.

"Can we have the menu cards please." He said to her as soon as she came to their table.

The waitress went to the cashier's desk and brought two, from the menu cards which were piled up. She came to Mike's table and gave one card to Mike and another to Mariella.

"I'm still getting the pizza; what are you ordering?" Mike asked Mariella.

"I think, I'll get a pizza as well, are you still going for the Margherita?" Mariella asked Mike.

"Yeah yeah and you the Capricciosa?" Mike asked Mariella to which she said yes.

Mike called the waitress to their table again and ordered a pizza for each of them. He also ordered a glass of wine for them to share. The waitress took the order and left one menu card at the table, took the other one and put it on top of the pile in the cashier's desk, entered details on the computer and went into the kitchen to give the order.

"So what happened Mike? Why did you want to see me all of a sudden?" Mariella asked Mike.

"Is it wrong that I want to see you?" Mike asked back.

"I didn't say that, and you know that yourself, tell me the real reason Mike." Mariella replied back.

"Straight to the point? How have we been doing in the past year? What's new with you and me? Seriously?" Mike smiled back as he asked this question.

"Well, I got a promotion and funnily enough I got it after I quit my current job, so they offered me a promotion to keep me there. I'm still deciding if I want to take it, things are great with Dad and the new boyfriend, it's early days but it's ok." Mariella said to Mike as she took a sip of wine.

"What about you Mike? Apart from solving cases and murder mysteries? Are you seeing someone finally?" she asked him.

"Well, first of all congrats! I'm really happy you're doing great and you're also with someone who is less complicated. I guess, you know how the case is going, and I am not seeing anyone serious. I tried, but I ended up with people with big time daddy issues. The last one was super jealous. Next one, yeah well, she had more red flags than the communist flag. So when she wanted to break up, I went along with it rather than trying to reason with her, so yeah, I think the case was having enough brain damage in me as it is, I didn't want to complicate it further. That's pretty much my work and dating life in the past year; all said and done, I am genuinely happy that you are doing better." Mike said as he drank some wine.

The waitress came with their order and served the two pizzas. She asked whether they need anything. Mike said no; the waiter smiled and went to attend another table nearby.

"Thanks for your concern Mike, but you never answered my initial question. Why did you want to meet? I need the real reason." Mariella asked Mike, while she was cutting her pizza into slices.

"Because I want to apologise, I wanted to say sorry for not being a husband when you needed one, because I just didn't know how. I feel bad for putting you through an emotional rollercoaster while we dated and got married. I just feel, have always felt that I never gave you closure even when you kept trying desperately to save whatever we had. That's on me, I was being a genuine dick, but I just want to let you know that sometimes I just didn't know how to act or react, and I'm not going to be blaming my past and all my childhood for my stupidity. As the days and weeks passed ever since we split, things have started to become more and more clear. It's now crystal clear where I messed up. I just want to own up to my share of mistakes.

"Mike, there were two people in that relationship; I wasn't perfect either. You weren't easy, but I wasn't perfect. I just wish you had been more open with your feelings, the way you are now. I'm just not sure the Mike from a year ago would even say whatever you just said a minute ago." Mariella replied to Mike.

"Well I can't keep pretending that I don't care or at least I can't keep doing that to people I care about. My obsession with things, especially having revenge at the back of my head for that fateful day, I was more a vengeful father than being a caring husband, even if you had come back from the dead with the severeness of that accident. Our marriage wasn't perfect, but I believe I pretty much nuked whatever was left in that marriage with the way I acted in the weeks following the accident. I don't know how much I hurt you back then, I am still not sure if I know even now. All I know is that I fucked up badly, and unfortunately you took it all. Again, I feel so sorry now. I know you act all friendly and you still try to make sure I'm ok, but if you still resent me for screwing up the relationship, I deserve every bit of it." Mike said to Mariella, looking at her, waiting to see her reaction.

"Mike, again, you need to stop blaming yourself for everything. I should have been more flexible with your decision making. You never really hid the fact that your social skills aren't really that great. Time and time again, I kept forgetting that I was dating and eventually married someone who grew up in an orphanage." Mariella said to Mike.

"That doesn't excuse the fact that I was being a complete dick head; I mean, I asked you to marry me." Mike replied to Mariella.

"And I said yes, I am responsible for that decision. All I'm saying is that you need to stop blaming yourself for what happened. I'm sorry I'm digging into your past Mike, but your mum left you when you were a toddler, your dad unfortunately died in a fire accident. You ended up in an orphanage even before you could understand what was happening around you. As much as Matteo was there to guide you as a mentor, you never really grew up with a family. This is you, you and that is something which only you can fix. You just need to get over whatever has been bothering you since your childhood and stop blaming yourself for whatever is going wrong now. I don't hate you now. I didn't hate you back then, I was frustrated, yes, but I could never hate you because your feelings in that relationship, good or bad, were never fake. You always were and still are the same person with everyone. The accident was not your fault, you took over that case because you wanted to. I was selfish enough to think you shouldn't, 'cause I wanted the relationship to work. But a lot of people in the city or even part of the country are sleeping safely because you took that case. Sure you made enemies, yes they did order a hit on you which made us lose our son before he was even born, but that is not your fault. The relationship? Would it have survived if you hadn't taken this case? Maybe? But would you have been happy if you didn't, the answer is no. This is all you know Mike, from the time in the orphanage, school and college, everything you did since your childhood was to be in this place you are now. I should have accepted that and shouldn't have thought that I could change you. This is you, this is who Michelangelo Costa is, I didn't understand that fully while being married. So yes, as much as you blame yourself, the same amount of blame goes for me as well. Maybe it's for the best, because even if the marriage ended, I haven't seen you this happy in a long time. I'm doing quite ok as well, am I sad that the marriage ended? Yes. But the end result was better for the both of us, even if it didn't make sense at that time." Mariella said to Mike who seemed a bit emotional. Mike didn't say anything for a minute or two while he kept tapping the table with his fingers while his eyes gave the impression that he was in deep thought and he was trying to say something.

"This is not how I expected this conversation to go, but these past few days have been a roller coaster, so I should have expected it on some levels." Mike said finally.

"I know, you thought that I needed some closure for our relationship, but in reality I was waiting to tell you this. You just were not in any frame to talk to me during this time and I waited for you to eventually reach out. Just so you would stop blaming yourself for everything." Mariella said to Mike as she held his hand.

"Thanks for saying this, it means a lot to me to know that you don't hate me. I mean, you get the point like hate in the sense of screwing up the relationship, you get the point. I don't even know how to say it now." Mike said as he mumbled and stumbled through the words.

"I know Mike, I know. My advice to you is don't let your personal feelings for us, which is a closed chapter already, blind you or your decision making in this case; this case is bigger than petty revenge, as the future of the country depends on it." Mariella said to Mike as she finished her food.

"Thanks for saying this, but it still would have been nice to have punched Alessio's face while he was still alive. Yes, yes, you can't have everything in life, I know." Mike said with a sheepish smile, trying to change the mood of the conversation.

"I know you would have. I need to go Mike, I need to run a few errands for the evening." Mariella said to Mike.

"Hey sure sure, thanks again for meeting me today. Do you need a lift?" Mike asked her.

"No, I drove here as well, don't worry." Marella said as she reached out to her purse.

"Hey, I've got the bill, it's fine, I insist. I invited you, this one's on me." Mike said as he went to the cashiers desk and paid the bill.

Mike and Mariella left the restaurant without saying much, but both of their faces had a sense of satisfaction on whatever they spoke of during lunch. Mike took out his pack of cigarettes and put one in his mouth.

“Mike, I know it’s none of my business, but at least try not to test how much your lungs can hold out, just friendly advice.” Mariella said as she hugged Mike.

“I’ll keep that in mind.” Mike nodded, taking the cigarette from his mouth and keeping it back into the pack.

Both of them stood hugging each other for a while before letting go. Mike walked Mariella to her car and waved her goodbye as she drove away. He went up to his car, took his phone out and sent a message to Matteo that he was going home.

Mike started the car, turned on his playlist from Spotify which contained a mixture of songs from Poets of The Fall, Metallica, Måneskin, Megadeth and Guns’n’Roses. Rather than taking the usual route, he drove towards the beach, with a smiling face and a sense of relief. The playlist switched to the song “ Fade to Black” from Metallica while he drove along the beach. As soon as the song started, Mike parked his car on the side of the road in one of the parking areas, opened the car center console and took out an envelope. He opened the envelope and took out a letter, it was an apology letter he had written to Mariella. He wanted to give this letter to her months ago but never did. He then took out the other paper from the envelope and it was a report of the termination of their unborn foetus. Maybe it was the song playing in the background along with it’s powerful lyrics; Mike remembered the time when he had suicidal tendencies. He took one huge breath and started smiling as he slid all the papers back in the envelope.

"Thank you for the memories, it was good while it lasted." He said, folded the envelope and started to tear it to dozens of tiny pieces. It was kind of a cinematic moment as "Fade to Black" solo was playing in the background.

He got out of the car, went to the nearest trash can and dropped the papers inside. He felt as if a huge weight had been lifted off his shoulders. He saw a cotton candy seller nearby, he went over to him and got himself a stick and started eating on the way back to his car. Mike looked at the beach and saw the families running around in the sand with whatever sun was left on a cloudy day, opened the car door and got inside. He saw that Matteo had tried calling him and also sent him a message.

Mike took his phone and saw the message; Matteo had sent him an image which had the full itinerary of Claudio for the next day, including the current evening. Mike noticed that Claudio was going to be at the Opera which was mentioned in the news earlier, the same event which was going to be attended by other big names in Naples and also from the country. Mike called Matteo back.

"I don't think it's a bad idea to have one of our guys at the Opera today." Mike said to Matteo.

"Why? Do you think something is going to happen? That place is going to be a fortress with all the security today." Matteo responded back.

"I guess it makes sense, I was just overthinking, my bad." Mike replied.

"You said you wanted an early day, what happened, took some drugs which was collected as evidence?" Matteo asked Mike.

"Nothing I just felt I needed to clear my head before going further on this case." Mike replied to Matteo.

"Do you care to elaborate?" Matteo asked Mike.

"I took your advice and met Mariella. Let's just say, both of us made our peace with the whole situation." Mike said to Matteo.

"Hmmm, ok that was something I didn't expect to hear from you, only thing I can say is. I'm proud of you, as long as you feel good, then I can safely assume you're finally starting to let go. Regarding work, I sent you some files, do check them out when you go home." Matteo said to Mike.

"I feel better, I'll talk about it when I'm ready. Anyways, do you want to give me a context of what I'm going to be looking at?" Mike asked.

"Cybersecurity came back; Enzo's phone was indeed being tapped. He had a Trojan in one of the applications he was using. Read the full report when you go home; it might help you with your meeting with Claudio tomorrow." Matteo said to Mike.

"Wow, just wow, as if this case wasn't mind-blowing already! I'll get to it when I'm home, I'll see you there as well in the evening, bye." Mike said as he disconnected the call.

Mike threw the phone on the passenger seat, finished his cotton candy, turned on the music and started driving towards Matteo's home. Mike kept thinking heavily while driving, razor focused on something. His face was completely different to the one he had when he came out of the restaurant and he was at the beach. Now that satisfaction and relief was gone, he had a touch of aggression in his eyes, as if he wanted to hit somebody. A complete 180 degree turn in human feelings. Mike entered Matteo's house using the spare keys which he had been given. He went into the kitchen, got himself a coffee mug and made some coffee. He also took a can of beer from the fridge and went towards the dining table. He kept the coffee and the beer on the table and took his laptop, turned it on and sat down. Mike went through the reports which Matteo had sent to him, he read that Enzo's phone had been hacked and every activity on his phone was being traced. From his movement to every location within five metres precisely, every text he has sent out, every WhatsApp conversation and even the apps which he had opened. Whoever hacked into Enzo's phone was keeping tabs on him for the past two months.

Mike went further into the report and read that Enzo's phone had been infected with a Trojan virus, as Matteo had said earlier. The Trojan was new, had been coded and created specifically for his phone. No codes of it even existed in any of the files the police had on records. It had either been transferred onto this phone through a public Wi-Fi network, file sharing or manually through a file uploaded on the device directly; there was no specific way to pinpoint how though. The report also concluded, this could be one way how everyone who was murdered had been picked up exactly, when they were alone or in private meetings. Matteo had also written a note at the end stating cybersecurity was evaluating the phones of all the deceased currently.

"Smart." Mike said to himself.

Mike had just taken out his phone and started writing something when he was suddenly interrupted by a phone call from Mario.

"So much for my early day off." Mike mumbled sarcastically to himself and answered the phone call.

"Mike, we've searched for bugs in Enzo's place and we've found nothing; it's a dead end." Mario said over the phone.

"Anything else that could be interesting? And hey, have you got any notification from Matteo?" Mike asked Mario.

"Yeah, he called a few minutes ago and mentioned the Trojan horse found on Enzo's phone."

"I think that pretty much solves it then. This guy or these guys; all the people involved in this are smarter than we estimated them to be." Mike replied, looking at the computer.

"Yeah true, why would you need to bug the house or any other places when you can virtually track and listen to everything through a person's smartphone, right?" Mario said to Mike.

"Yeah, I admire this to be honest, turning something in our possession against us. For all of our sake, let's hope this is just one person we are dealing with; I still have the feeling there are multiple people involved. The hacker could just be part of the group." Mike said to Mario.

"I hear you on that." Mario said to Mike.

"Hey Mario, before we finish off, can you make sure that security is absolutely tight at the Opera today? They said it'd be a fortress but I wouldn't mind you guys taking a look again." Mike replied to Mario.

"We can do that; we're close by anyway. I will check it out. I hope, whatever you wanted to do in the afternoon went well, though." Mario said to Mike.

"Thanks, buddy, it was great. Honestly, I'm thinking of going to sleep taking a pill just so I don't get woken up by the sudden calm in my brain." Mike replied to Mario.

"That's a weird reason to actually take a sleeping pill, but whatever works for you and good luck for tomorrow." Mario said to Mike.

"Thanks, Mario, I'll see you later." Mike said to Mario disconnecting the call.

Mike closed his laptop and went outside to the garden and took a walk around the property. He then went to his car, opened the door and got a bottle of pills he had in the car's center console. He looked at the watch in his hand and saw the time was around 4PM.

"It's been a while since I slept for more than 12 hours." He said to himself as he looked at the pills.

Mike walked back into the house, entered the bedroom, then turned around and looked at the TV. He picked up a blanket from the bed and went back to the couch and turned on the TV. He put Netflix on and played 'Tear Along the Dotted Line' [Strappare lungo i bordi]. He took a pill and started watching the series. By the time Matteo came home, the series was already playing its last episode and Mike was snoring on the couch.

"Jesus Christ, and I thought he might just be binge drinking to celebrate being happy." Matteo said as he saw Mike's sleeping pills on the table near the couch. He went over to the table, took the TV remote and turned it off. Mike's legs and arms were all over the place; Matteo put Mike in a good sleeping position, covering him with the blanket and turned off the light in the main hall. He went into the kitchen, took some food from the fridge, came outside to the stairs, looked at Mike who was in deep sleep, snoring but with a certain calm in his face which Matteo hadn't seen in a while, and he smiled and went upstairs to his room.

Buzz buzzzzzzz buuuuzzzzzzzz

Mike's phone started buzzing with his automatic alarm set to ring everyday at 7AM. He woke up and sat with his hand on his head; he looked around and realised the time.

'God, that's the new personal record, close to 14 hours, now I know how cats feel." He thought to himself as he picked up his phone.

Mike got up from the couch and made his way to the kitchen. He got himself a glass and filled it with some tap water and drank it. After that he made his way towards the coffee maker, filled it with fresh beans and made himself a double espresso. He took a cigarette from his pack, took the coffee mug and went to the garden and stood there in the sun with a coffee mug in one hand and a cigarette in the other. He walked around the garden until he finished smoking and went to the orange tree and got himself a fruit. Mike started walking back into the house and kept the coffee mug in the sink, peeled the orange and started eating the fruit and made his way upstairs to Matteo's room. He noticed Matteo was not in bed and he could see the bathroom door was locked. He went back downstairs and made his way to the shower. By the time Mike was out, Matteo was already at the dining table, all dressed up with a coffee and a sandwich before him.

"One day the world is going to run out of water and you're going to be one of the major reasons for it." Matteo said to Mike.

"Everyone has a guilty pleasure." Mike replied as he walked towards his room.

"All I'm saying is maybe you should stop masturbating in the shower. It might save some water, and you won't be late to work." Matteo said to Mike with a straight poker face.

"Thank you, I will keep that in mind next time." Mike responded as he shut the door.

Mike was out in a few minutes, dressed sharply from his side as he was checking through the messages from last night. He was reading about the Opera and was checking the entire timeline of the event. Nothing of note had happened like he had feared, which was good.

"You don't know where you're meeting Claudio, right?" Matteo asked Mike sarcastically.

"Right after the service of his waste of sperm brother, outside the cemetery. Have I missed something?" Mike responded to Matteo.

"Nope, just try to get as much as details as possible, you got one shot." Matteo said to Mike.

"Got it. What are you going to do in the office today? Whose balls is Domenico busting now?" Mike asked Matteo.

"Twenty-five kilos of cocaine was found at Enzo's house; he is just trying to establish where that was going to go. After you're done with Claudio, we will see if we can find further links on what is happening." Matteo responded.

"I'll make a move then; I'll see you at the precinct when it's over." Mike made his way out of the house and towards his car.

He looked at his watch and got into the car, put on his sunglasses, played his Spotify playlist again from his mobile, through the car's bluetooth speakers and started driving towards the cemetery. While on his way and standing at the traffic lights, he looked outside the car and saw a married couple in the car next to him with the woman talking to her kids in the backseat, husband at the wheel. The lights turned green and Mike continued towards his destination. He reached the location as the service was still ongoing at the church; the cemetery was about two-hundred metres away from the church, but the entire property belonged to the parish.

"I wonder if all this prayer is still going to make a difference for someone of his sort, when he's already dead." Mike murmured while getting out of the car.

Mike noticed that Claudio's security guys were standing outside the church in full force. He went in and noticed the place was almost full. Interestingly enough, some of the big names at the previous night's opera attended the service in memory of Vincenzo. Mike hadn't been to church for months, it took a few seconds for him to find a seat at the back, and he sat there silently watching the proceedings. Mike listened to the Priest praying for the dead soul, Claudio's speech recalling good moments of Vincenzo's life, making people in attendance laugh a bit as well. Mike eventually got restless after seeing what he felt as a farce and went outside the church. He took out his phone, put on his headphones and started playing his online game from earlier, while keeping an eye on the service inside the church.

Mike got a text message while he was on his phone to go to the cemetery and wait for Claudio. Mike read the text, looked around and he noticed one of the security guards near the door of the church was looking at him and shook his head implying he's to go to the cemetery. Mike just nodded his head and went to the cemetery and waited at the entrance. The service was already coming to an end when Mike got the text, so after a few minutes Claudio came to the cemetery accompanied by four guards. He saw Mike at the entrance and came up to him, while the guards stayed behind.

"Let's go inside Mike. Have you paid respect to my brother?" Claudio asked Mike, who simply looked at Claudio without saying a word.

Claudio and Mike started walking inside the cemetery accompanied by two of his guards while the other two stood outside.

"So Mr. Michelangelo Costa, have you found out who murdered my brother?" Claudio asked.

"We're working on it, and I was hoping you'd be able to tell me who I should consider as a person of interest in the murders of Silvio, Alessio and Enzo?" Mike responded and questioned Claudio.

"Isn't that your job, Captain Michelangelo?" Claudio responded to Mike with disgust.

"Ohhh it is, that's why I'm talking to someone who I suspect could be behind these murders as revenge for his brother." Mike shot back at Claudio.

"Careful with your words and tone, Captain. If I wanted them gone, I wouldn't have waited for a month after my brother's murder to take care of them." Claudio said to Mike, his tone getting more cynical.

"So why did you want to meet me privately? Mike asked Claudio.

"Just to tell you and your department, that you have maybe one month to find whoever is behind the murder of my brother and also Silvio, Alessio and Enzo." Claudio said. He looked absolutely calm; his words lacked anger or frustration, yet his eyes gave a very different picture. They were the eyes of the Devil's messenger, a sneak peek to burning hell, with the promise of eternal damnation.

"Well, we're not exactly scratching our balls here. Listen, I want to know! What was your brother's plan in regards to the migrants? Asking Silvio and Alessio to slow down or stop regular activity as a whole, until the elections were over, had caused problems between all of you right? What can you tell me about that? What can you tell me about your beef with the Albanian mafia? Who is after you in the Sicilian mafia? What can you tell me about the cocaine found at Enzo's house?" Mike asked Claudio whose face turned colours as his displeasure grew.

"Who do you think you are, Michelangelo? I called you here because I wanted to tell you at my brother's grave that I will avenge his death. I didn't call you here to answer your questions. You have one month to find who is behind all this, so I can chop off their heads and decorate them as ornaments on top of my brothers grave." Claudio said to Mike with a sense of calm, but his eyes painted a different picture.

"And what happens if it takes more than a month to find out who is behind all this?" Mike questioned Claudio again.

“Naples would need to get ready for a bloodbath.” Claudio answered, without thinking for even a second.

“Maybe this is why old people should stay away from politics.” Mike responded to Claudio.

“I believe my message has been delivered, you’re no longer of any use to me now, so get out of my sight. The clock is ticking, Captain Michelangelo Costa.” Claudio said to Mike.

“I still need an answer for my question, old man. Do you want me to find these people? Fine. Then answer me.”

“Do you think I wouldn’t answer if it could solve this? Well it won’t, that’s why I’m not even wasting a second to answer your stupid theories. Now, get going.” Claudio said to Mike and called the two guards inside the cemetery, who came close to Mike.

“Throw him out.” Claudio said to the guards, his body giving the vibe of indifference to Mike being there..

“You don’t get to.......” Mike started speaking, but he felt a sting on his neck and fell down backwards. As he was losing consciousness, he felt blood splatter on his face, someone had fallen on his feet. He heard a few faint gunshots but lost consciousness while seeing the silhouette of a person getting close to Claudio.

8

The Mystery Killer

Mike woke up in a hospital bed with IV fluids being given to him; Matteo and Lorenzo were inside the hospital room and he heard a lot of commotion outside. Mike felt groggy and saw his colleagues had noticed that he was awake.

"What the hell happened? How have I made it here? Where the heck is Claudio?" Mike bombarded Matteo and Lorenzo with questions when his memories came back to him.

"We were hoping you would tell us what happened." Matteo said to Mike looking at him.

"That I would tell you what happened? Wait. What happened, how did you guys find me at the cemetery?" Mike asked Matteo, surprised.

"Mike, seriously! You don't remember anything? Do you remember anything before you passed out?" Lorenzo asked Mike.

"I just remember a sting on my neck; I fell back and… there were gunshots and someone came running towards Claudio.. Wait, is he alive? What the fuck happened to that bastard?" Mike asked both Matteo and Lorenzo.

"He got Claudio, that's what's happened." Matteo said to Mike, explaining the situation

"Got him? As in kidnapped Claudio? Or is he dead?" Mike replied back, banging the bed with his fist.

"Claudio is dead; you were the only survivor, because he hit you with a nerve toxin placed dart. Each of the guards got a bullet in the head. Claudio's body in the meantime was picked up in an abandoned car near the Catacombs of San Gennaro." Matteo said to Mike.

"Boy, he has a wicked sense of humour, leaving a dead body near a burial ground! How long have I been unconscious?" Mike asked his colleagues.

"Almost a day." Lorenzo replied.

'It seems the killer didn't want to kill you; he ensured you were only disabled but made sure everyone else was dead. Claudio was tortured like the others, dead by punctured lungs; it must have been painful. But it didn't end before he was severely beaten, getting a few broken bones in the arms and legs." Matteo said to Mike.

"Jesus Christ, what kind of psychopaths did these guys end up pissing off in the past, talk about karma catching up with you with a vengeance?" Mike said as he looked at Matteo and Lorenzo.

"Pandora's box seems to have been opened again." Lorenzo said.

"What did we find from the crime scene, any evidence left?" Mike asked.

"The bullets were from a.45 caliber; forensics concluded that the pistol was HK5 with a suppressor. The two guards outside the cemetery also had the same bullet marks from the same weapon. For you, he has used a nerve gas, mixed it with some other chemical compound. That's why you didn't have a fatal reaction, but killing you wasn't his intention, like we mentioned before. He used a dart gun for you. Mike, we need you to think and remember; there must be something which you had left out without your knowledge. Some unimportant details that could get us closer, anything. Get some rest and think it through. I'll handle the press and people who want our heads from the politicians side for brownie points in the meantime." Matteo said to Mike as he and Lorenzo started to make their way out of the room.

"Handle the press? What do you mean?" Mike asked, trying to understand the situation.

"It means that bodies are in the same hospital and media persons are swarming like vultures for any news they can get. You'll see when you look outside your window. Happens when someone running in the next election is murdered and his body is found near a National Landmark" Matteo said to Mike, explaining the situation.

"Where are the others?" Mike asked again.

"Mario and Federico are with forensics. By the way, Mariella was here last evening to check on you and so was that neighbour of yours. What was her name, maybe Rita? Yeah, Rita. She was here with her kid to check on you. Just try to get back to them, maybe they texted you or something." Lorenzo responded.

"How long before I can get out of this bed?" Mike asked Matteo who was leaving as well.

"I'll send the doctor here; you should rest Mike." Matteo said.

Mike saw his phone was on the side of the bed, picked it up with his other hand and checked the news. The entire country was talking about the death of Claudio, it was only natural to assume a person of his standing and someone who was almost nailed on to win a post in the Italian cabinet in the upcoming election, got this much attention. There seemed to be a few voices on social media though, who seemed to be happy that this gangster wasn't going to be a policy maker in the country. There seemed to be fans of whoever the killer was, some started giving vigilante names to this mysterious person or gang operating behind these murders. While Mike kept scrolling on his phone, the doctor, along with a nurse, entered the room.

"How do you feel, Mr. Michelangelo?" He asked Mike while he came and checked on the reports which were written and hung near the bed.

"Good, pretty good. Only, it would be nice to know what happened in the past day and would also be nice to know when I can get out of this bed." Mike replied back.

"Your vitals seem normal; I believe you can be leaving in a few hours. We're going to run one more test to make sure that the toxin shot into you cannot do any further damage." The doctor said to Mike.

"What was I hit with? Any idea?" Mike asked the doctor.

"He's used different nerve toxins from fish. What are they mixed with? We do not know, he found a perfect combination to make sure you're only disabled. We have asked to find out what toxins were there in your bloodstream. We will be able to give you that report later in the day before you leave." The doctor responded.

"So this guy knows his chemicals and how to use them? Interesting." Mike replied to the doctor.

"Thanks for the details doctor." He added further.

"Seems like it Michelangelo, they definitely know how to use chemicals." The doctor said to Mike while the nurse took a blood sample from Mike from his right hand, and she removed the IV drips and the tubes connected to him.

"So is that food still good to eat and is it okay for me to move around from the bed?" Mike asked the doctor.

"It should be, but do not attempt to move much and please rest, we still want to confirm you are going to be ok, we have your blood samples. Eat and get some rest again, Mr Michelangelo, I'll see you later in the day." The doctor said, leaving along with the nurse as Mike started to eat.

Mike took the plate in his hand and went close to the window. He looked outside and saw a bunch of police officers on the ground floor, and also a few reporters standing at a distance with cameras and microphones in their hands. Mike kept the plate down and took his phone and opened his messages. Like Lorenzo had said earlier, he had received texts from Mariella and Rita and other acquaintances. He started walking up and down in the room, texting each one of them while occasionally stopping by the plate to take a bite. He wrote to Mariella that he was grateful for the conversation two days ago and said he was happy to know she had visited him. He wrote Rita he was alright and he would contact her as soon as he was outside the hospital.

"Hey, I just can't seem to get out of trouble lately; you should tell me how your date went the other day. I hope, there hasn't been any further packages you had to collect for me on my behalf, if you already did, thanks and sorry at the same time as always." Mike wrote back to her.

Mike went to the window once more and saw the crowd outside while having the food tray in his hand. He was using the wall as support as he leaned with his shoulder looking at the sky, the roads and everything outside in general, when suddenly he saw a group of Napoli fans running in the street. Mike realised there was a football match that day between Napoli and Juventus, with Naples playing host to one of their bitter rivals. He finished the food, got the tray away and turned on the TV. He tuned to the sports channel and put on the match, just in time for kick-off. He took the medication pills which were left for him by the doctor and ate them while drinking a glass of water. Mike spent the next two hours watching the match intently, with no winners coming out of it. Heated exchanges between players, red cards and physical shoving and fan violence inside the stadium. The match had ended on a goalless draw, but the off field and post-match antics took more spotlight than the match itself.

"Everyone in the city wants to fight these days, I wonder what would have happened if Napoli had lost? Maybe Mt.Vesuvius would have erupted." Mike said to himself, while turning off the TV and closing his eyes trying to get some sleep.

Mike suddenly woke up from his bed hearing a scream outside this room, he heard a gunshot and more and more gunshots were heard with the sound coming closer and closer to his room. He heard another woman screaming and he jumped out of bed. He could not find a thing in the hospital that could have been useful to fight against guns, but he did take a flower vase and went out of the room just when a gun was pointed right on his head.

"You're next Captain Michelangelo Costa, you think you could hide forever?" Mike saw a masked man surrounded by several of his men who were looking directly at him, one of them had Federico kneeling down next to him, executing him right in front of Mike's eyes. The man then said to him he was next.

"Let's see who's next." Mike thought to himself, while lunging forward at the men, the entire image started to shake and the men were all becoming distorted with Mike hearing faint voices before it became loud and clear.

"Mike, Mike, wake up." Federico stood next to Mike, when Mike opened his eyes.

"What happened?" Mike asked Federico, while wiping his forehead, noticing he was sweating all over.

"You were having a dream or nightmare, I think; and you started mumbling random words. What the hell did you dream?" Federico asked Mike, trying to find out what disturbed Mike this much.

"There was a shootout in the hospital, you got executed right outside this room and I was shot right after that before you woke me up." Mike said to Federico, while clearing out the sweat in his face. He got out of bed.

"Do you have to be violent, dark and depressed even in your dreams?" Federico asked Mike while he threw a towel at him.

"Do you think I said ten hail Marys to have a nightmare before I went to bed? What's the status of Claudio's autopsy? What's the drama I'm missing outside this room?" Mike asked Federico while Mario, Lorenzo and Matteo along with the doctor and two nurses came inside Mike's room.

"Hello Michelangelo, how are you feeling? Did you manage to get rest?" The doctor asked Mike while coming near the bed.

"All good, doctor, all good. I was just getting bored lying in bed all day. Did you find any issue in my blood report? Am I good enough to leave?" Mike asked the doctor as he came and sat down in the bed.

"You are safe Mike, there's not much to worry, though we would request you to get some rest and stay home for a couple of days and continue the medication. just as a precaution." the doctor said to Mike.

"That's going to be a bit difficult in the current scenario, but I'll try. Can I have the report of what toxins I was injected with? It would be helpful for the investigation which we're dealing with." Mike said.

"Well I have it Mike, I got it right here." Matteo said to Mike holding on to a file.

"That's fast, so what was a I hit with?" Mike asked Matteo, trying to find an answer.

"From what we read and what the doctor and the lab technicians told us, it's a venom with a mixture of curare, puffer fish and jellyfish. So Tetrodotoxin in major levels, accompanied by other agents. He's created a new compound which might be useful for our military in future for covert operations, if you ask me." Matteo responded to Mike.

"Good to know I was the test bunny, unless he used it earlier on someone else." Mike looked at the ceiling, saying the words while shaking his head, giving the impression he was trying to guess the answer and hoping it was true.

"That's exactly what you're going to do for the next day while sitting at home." Matteo said to Mike.

"So I'm leaving now? Am I good to go doctor?" Mike asked while turning his attention to the doctor.

"Yes, Michelangelo. I've said that earlier, you can leave, just try not to push yourself too much." The doctor replied to Mike.

"Sorry, maybe I just misunderstood, I assumed that I was leaving in another hour or two. Thank you, doctor." Mike replied to the doctor and shook his hand.

"You're welcome, Michelangelo." The doctor said to Mike, he shook the hand of Mike's colleagues and left the room with the nurses.

"Here, thought you might need this." Matteo gave Mike a bag, which had a fresh shirt inside.

"I definitely need this." Mike said while getting up from bed and started changing his shirt.

"So what kind of shitstorm am I stuck in?" Mike asked Matteo while the others looked on.

"Fortunately, not much. Just that the media is having a field day, they're talking about police ineptitude in solving this case, even if the people aren't afraid, these guys sure as hell want them to be." Matteo said to Mike.

"I mean, mass media in 2020's, what did you expect? Anyways, so I'm staying home and doing what?" Mike asked Matteo, trying to find out his task further.

"Trying to find the missing links; like the doctor said you need to be resting for a day or two, so just rest and sit on the couch or lie down in bed and analyse this case, whatever there is to be found, and try to find a link somewhere. In the meantime, we will be out in the field and dig further and further." Matteo said to Mike.

"It won't be a bad idea for you to maybe meet a few people, who are worried about you and showed up at the hospital." Federico added further.

"Yeah yeah, I hear you guys." Mike responded while he finished getting dressed.

"Who has my car keys? Or did it fall down somewhere while I was knocked out?" Mike asked the team, checking his pockets.

"Your car is safely parked at my house Mike, you're coming with me. Let's go." Matteo said to Mike, asking him to make a move.

"Ok, sure. I just asked a question; you don't need to be rude, I am still an outpatient." Mike replied to Matteo while getting out of the room with Matteo rolling his eyes, Mario and Lorenzo looking at each other and Federico facepalming himself.

"You three call it a day as well. It's about time you guys got some sleep, too. We'll meet tomorrow at the precinct and decide what we do next." Matteo said to Lorenzo, Mario and Federico.

"Sure, boss, see you tomorrow then." they said to Matteo and left the hospital room together.

Matteo noticed Mike was standing in the balcony looking outside, the Press and all the police vehicles downstairs, while occasionally texting. Mike saw Matteo coming towards him and turned around keeping his phone inside his pocket. While all the others in the team were leaving on the opposite side of the room.

“What’s the situation with Domenico, did he say anything about this whole mess?” Mike asked Matteo.

“What can he say? I mean, he’s pissed that Claudio’s dead and of course, whoever we are after is on a killing spree, we still don’t know if it is one person or multiple people. So he has to deal with the politicians making lousy statements to the media, while getting roasted himself in the process. It is what it is. Although, now he seemed happy to know that you and Mariella finally spoke to each other, getting some sort of closure, both of you.” Matteo replied, as they kept walking towards the parking lot.

“There should be a link, I’m still trying to piece together what happened at the cemetery. Let me go through the reports and data from forensics, something might click in my head. Maybe that might open up something we have been missing all this time and failed to see earlier.” Mike said to Matteo.

“We’re still trying to figure out where and how he came to the cemetery to pick Claudio, right under the noses of his own security. This guy has planned everything to the last details.” Matteo said to Mike as they reached his car.

Matteo and Mike got into the car; Matteo took the wheel driving both of them outside the hospital. They exchanged words on what happened at the hospital, in regards to the press conference which Domenico had held yesterday, when and what time Mariella and Rita had come to the hospital to check up on Mike, what Domenico had told Matteo about the conversation Mike had with Mariella, the autopsy reports of Claudio and his guards, and by the time they reached Matteo's house they got started on the topic of what happened in the cemetery.

"You know what's really surprising in all this?" Mike asked Matteo.

"What? Please try not to make a dark joke." Matteo warned Mike, while getting out of the car.

"Ok, I'll skip the joke. Seriously, I'm still asking your opinion; we might be dealing with multiple people helping one specific executioner or maybe two executioners." Mike said to Matteo.

"Based on the killing pattern?" Matteo asked Mike while he opened the door to the house.

"Yeah, I mean, just take a look at it. Silvio, Alessio, Vincenzo and Claudio. The way these guys were murdered was brutal, absolute carnage and torture. It sort of seems these guys had history and a lot of debt to be paid, which didn't really pay off to our dead men when the tide's changed, atleast not the way they wanted for sure. Then there is the case of Enzo, one single shot to the head by a qualified sniper. There is me, not killed but disabled. Add the four guards at the cemetery who were taken out in close combat by a silenced pistol. There has to be at least two or three people being involved here. Because otherwise, it is sort of a miracle what this guy is pulling, if this is one single person behind all this. Think of hacking all of the phones, like creating a new trojan horse by himself. That's something." Mike said to Matteo while putting in some coffee beans and switching on the coffee maker.

"Do you need one as well?" He asked Matteo.

"Yeah sure. I have some leftover grilled chicken and vegetables. Do you want to cook or shall we order something?" Matteo asked Mike.

"Hmmm, that seems to be almost a whole chicken; I think we can eat that after you heat it up." Mike said to Matteo after inspecting the contents of Matteo's fridge.

Matteo heated up the chicken and the vegetables while Mike made two coffees, a double espresso for himself and a single espresso for Matteo. The food was ready in a few minutes and Mike had already set up the table, brought the coffee to the table along with a beer from the cooler in the hall.

"So, what are you guys planning to do tomorrow? I mean, I know my role for the next two days. I'm just curious what you guys are going to dig through." Mike asked Matteo, while they both started having dinner.

"The same thing I told you at the hospital; we're going to try to ruffle some feathers in Claudio's circle and see if something happens. We would also need to check the church where the service was happening and we're checking the personnel list, because this guy seems to have come out of nowhere and took all of you out. I'm thinking maybe he was masquerading as one of the security guards." Matteo said to Mike.

"To think that about a week ago I was on an official suspension, now we're having dinner discussing four murders which happened within this short time. Whoever said life is unpredictable, was definitely not kidding." Mike said to Matteo, sort of reflecting the past week.

"I hear what you're saying. Have you watched the match today?" Matteo asked Mike.

"Yeah, I watched it before falling asleep in the hospital. It wasn't the best match, at least it had drama," Mike said to Matteo, smirking.

"We could use less drama lately." Matteo mumbled.

"Let's toast to it, to less drama." Mike lifted his coffee mug in the air sarcastically as Matteo did the same with his beer planking the glass and beer can together.

"Are you done eating, by the way?" Matteo asked Mike while keeping the can down.

"Yeah, you finish the beer, I will take the dishes." Mike said to Matteo, and he started arranging the plates in his hands and grabbed the coffee mugs and took them to the kitchen sink.

While Mike was placing the dishes in the sink, Matteo came to the kitchen with his beer in his hand and stood by the kitchen table. Mike turned around and instantly knew Matteo wanted to say something.

"What is it? Is something wrong?" Mike asked Matteo, trying to find out what was running in his head.

"I'm happy you survived yesterday, especially after what seemed like a huge load off your chest the day before to Mariella. I don't want to know what you guys spoke of, I'm just happy that you are finally starting to feel better in your heart and in your head. With that in mind, I'm really happy nothing happened to you yesterday at the cemetery." Matteo said to Mike, trying to keep as straight a face as possible.

"Likewise, thanks for sticking with me all along, not just the past few days, but from the time you took me under your wing at the orphanage. Honestly, I don't think I would have spoken to Mariella if you hadn't suggested that I talk the other day. I might have still been on my shell and and just continued how I was before without knowing her true feelings, because I was afraid to hear what she felt." Mike said to Matteo, looking at the floor, occasionally giving him eye contact but generally looking away, as he was getting mental images of the past in his head.

"You don't need to thank me Mike, I did what I could and I still do what I can because you're still that same kid who was erratic but with high potential. It was good to see that kid finally turning into a man, still erratic but still with a lot of potential. But you remained a kid when it came to your past. What you're doing now, letting it go or at least trying to as I understand, you might finally get to see the world in a different way and maybe your friends and relationships in a different way." Matteo said to Mike, still standing near the table.

'I know or I think I know, but thanks for telling me this and again, thanks for sticking around with me all along." Mike said to Matteo looking at him this time maintaining eye contact directly.

Matteo went to the trash can and threw the empty beer tin inside it and he went over to Mike and gave him a hug for a few seconds without saying anything. He then turned around without saying a word and started walking but stopped at the entrance of the kitchen and looked at Mike.

"I don't want to play matchmaker, but that girl living next door to your house, Rita, correct? She seems nice and her kid, she's gorgeous." Matteo said to Mike and he continued walking towards the stairs.

"You know if you're trying to sound mysterious, you actually suck at it, at least when you're giving me love advice." Mike said to Matteo with a smile on his face.

"I'm a man in his 50s, I can only say things as I know, this is how I did until now and I didn't suggest anything, mind you." Matteo said to Mike while continuing to walk up the stairs to reach his room.

"Sure, absolutely sure old man. Goodnight." Mike said to Matteo as he heard the door shut from his room.

"It's like I can't hide anything from this guy these days, though. I don't think he was wrong about anything though." Mike said to himself.

Mike came out of the kitchen, while getting himself a glass of water. He went to the bag he brought with himself from the hospital and opened it. He took the medication which was given to him and removed the pills from its cover and ate them. He went to the main door and made sure it was locked, and then he made his way towards his room. He was reading the news for a while on his phone when he got a text from Rita answering his message earlier.

"Hey, good to hear you are ok. I couldn't see you at the hospital because you were still unconscious and yes there was one package which arrived and it's safe with me. The date was ok, but I didn't feel a connection so there was no follow-up."

"Yeah I'm good, I was told to rest for a couple of days, so I'm going to be working from Matteo's house, investigating forensic reports from the previous murders and trying to match it up with the current one. Thanks for the package and bummer for the date, but I don't want to sound like a nut. Would you be interested in having dinner with me sometime when this chaos is over?" Mike texted back.

"We can have dinner on Friday night, even if your case is not over. Why don't you come over?" Rita wrote back to Mike.

"Friday night it is." Mike replied.

"Do you have any special requests for dinner or any specific cuisine?" Rita wrote back again.

"Whatever works and is easier for you."

"Ok, I'll see you on Friday, goodnight then, Mike." Rita read and finished the conversation for the day with a smiley.

"Good night then, take care." Mike wrote back, giving a smile all through the conversation.

9

CLUES AND THE CULPRIT?

Mike turned off the alarm on his phone and put it on aeroplane mode and went to sleep. Next morning when he woke up the time was close to 9AM. He got out of bed and walked out to the hallway only to find an emptied coffee mug at the dining table and Matteo's work shoes missing from the shoe holder at the entrance. He figured Matteo had already left to work. Mike made himself a coffee, a double espresso. He drank it in one shot and went into the bathroom to take a shower. Mike came back outside wrapped in a towel and made himself a salad with the vegetables he could find in the fridge. He took the salad to the dining table and went back to the coffee machine and made himself another double espresso. Mike finished his meal while replying to the messages he had received over the past two days. He then got dressed in some pyjamas and opened his laptop.

Mike started reading the reports from the forensics department related to Claudio's murder, first reading the entire findings from the cemetery during his abduction and how Mike was found unconscious. He read further into what the forensics found in connection with the murder of the guards and how the killer had made his way through without being noticed by anyone. Next, he started studying how Claudio's body was found inside a car, the exact details and injuries found on his body. The patterns again seemed consistent with all the previous murders as Mike had thought and said earlier to his team. He was going through the photographs of the entire events from the cemetery to the car. He analysed the reports of every murder which had happened, from Vincenzo, Alessio and Silvio. Mike then took a look at the photographs of all the murders and the area and the surroundings which were snapped by forensics in their report, and that's when something caught his eye in the material related to Silvio's murder.] There was a boot print he found close to the window; it wasn't a full footprint, it had only half a shoe's print marked in blood. Mike was able to find the same footprint in the car in which Claudio was found, with mud marks on the passenger seat. He pulled out the photos from the cemetery and saw footprints in multiple places on the wet grassy surface, but everything belonged to one single person. Mike then started reading all the reports again, focusing on the size of the footprints and what was written about them.

One of the reports caught the eyes of Mike specifically; it mentioned that the shoe was most likely therapeutic shoes. This was the one from Silvio's murder. Mike started checking who was at the church during Vincenzo's service held by Claudio. He was making his own notes of the entire situation and was convinced that there had to be someone as influential as Claudio in the church who was relaying information to the killer. The execution was flawless as regards Claudio's abduction from the cemetery. It needed pinpoint precision and planning and absolute certainty what Claudio and Mike was going to do. Based on Mike's own mental images before his blackout and four and six reports, he tried to recreate the situation from the footprints and the dead bodies. Claudio's abduction from the cemetery lasted less than two minutes, including getting Claudio out of the cemetery without being seen by anyone in the vicinity, which again had to be planned and executed flawlessly because there were still people around the church and in its premises when it all played out. Mike was trying to find a connection to the footprint and the therapeutic shoes, which he believed was a major clue for this case. While cross-referencing the lists of people, based on some major cases in the past, he had identified earlier who could have been behind the murders. Mike was able to pinpoint one specific person, who fit the description based on the shoes and the footprint from Claudio's murder scene in the car. Filippo Patrizi, the billionaire socialite with anisomelia, who wore speciality shoes for his condition on his right leg.

Mike verified an important detail during Claudio's abduction; Filippo had kept the crowd engaged in the church when service was over, which covered the time frame the killer had taken at the cemetery. Mike dug through some other records for more and more details going through Filippo's files. Even though he was a respected socialite, he was known for his friendships with people on the dark side. There were always persistent rumours that he was involved in dark and shady businesses but nothing was ever proved. His image not only in Naples but Italy as a whole was big, especially for his work with the disabled, the homeless and working for migrant rights, always played out in his advantage. This was also the reason why he was added to the list of individuals, which Mike and his colleagues took over as a secret investigation almost two years ago.

Mike initiated a phone call to his entire team while cross checking references, keeping his eyes glued on the computer.

"Mike, a group call? What happened? Everything ok?" Matteo asked Mike.

"What if I told you that I have a suspect in my head, and it seems to me that he is very capable in pulling off whatever has happened until now?" Mike said to the group.

"So here's the thing, me and Lorenzo are parked on the side of the road because you called, so do you have anything?" Federico said to Mike.

" I am..." Mario started talking.

"No one cares, Mike, what did you find?" Matteo interrupted Mario and asked Mike in a stern manner, asking him to explain what he had in mind without beating around the bush.

"A footprint, a specific footprint which are almost identical or I would just call it identical found in the murder of Silvio and Claudio in the car." Mike said to everyone who was listening.

"You say a footprint? Like what footprint are we talking about?" Matteo asked Mike.

"Listen, I know this sounds crazy but I think Filippo Patrizi is our guy, or he's the mastermind or atleast, someway involved in this big time." Mike said to Matteo and the others in a serious tone.

"Filippo Patrizi? How? How, I understand he is on our list of people who we are keeping track of, but him? Especially the mastermind? Mike you better have a solid reason behind all this." Matteo said to Mike.

"Why don't you all come here? To Matteo's house, so I can actually show you what I found and we can discuss here how we can take this further." Mike asked the team.

"We're already on the way, so we can take a detour and be there by 4PM?" Lorenzo responded to Mike.

"Mario and Matteo, how about you guys?" Mike asked.

"Well I'm on the way to the precinct, but sure, I can just drive there directly. How about you boss?" Mario responded to Mike and asked Matteo.

"So everyone invited themselves and I'm the last one to actually say that I will make it to my own house, good. we all meet there by 4PM then?" Matteo asked everyone over the phone.

"Yeah 4PM. should be fine, we'll see you there." Lorenzo responded over the phone, while Federico started driving the car through the traffic.

"I'm on my way there 4PM should be fine." Mario replied and disconnected the call.

"Mike, get all the details ready by the time we're there." Matteo responded and disconnected the call.

Mike started to take a notepad and started writing and drawing something, occasionally looking at the computer and switching between tabs on the computer screen. Hours had passed and Mike barely moved from the couch he had been sitting on since the morning. Mike heard the gate open outside and figured Matteo was the first one to arrive. He still did not get up and just continued to write on the Notepad. Matteo's car stopped, but Mike heard two more vehicles arriving at the property and knew that his entire team was here. He got up from the couch, took his laptop and notepad and went to the television to connect the laptop to the external cables and went to the front door. By the time Mike was halfway there Matteo had opened the door and entered the house followed by Lorenzo, Federico and Mario.

"Are you guys hungry? Because I am, I've completely forgotten that I haven't eaten anything since morning and haven't realised either that I haven't even got up from the couch." Mike said to the team looking at them, waited a second before going towards the fridge.

"Sure, Mike, you've knocked yourself out badly this time." Matteo said to Mike.

"Do you guys need a coffee?" Matteo asked the remaining three.

"Sure, I could do with one and I believe, the same goes for Mario as well; he's already nodding his head." Federico said to Matteo.

"I'm good, boss, I think I'll just take a couple of fruit from here." Lorenzo said to Matteo while he took a banana and a peach from the tray Matteo had at the dining table.

Mike cut one slice of bread and ate it with a glass of water, then took a pill which he had in his pocket, prescribed to him at the hospital earlier. He came outside the kitchen and noticed everyone was looking at him while they were drinking their coffee or eating their fruit, sitting on the couch and the chairs close to where Mike had set up the laptop to the television.

"Are you good?" Matteo asked Mike.

"Yeah, I just needed something to eat and to get some sugar in my body." Mike responded to Matteo.

"So then go ahead, what did you find and how did you come to the conclusion Filippo Patrizi could be the main man based on a footprint?" Matteo said to Mike.

Mike opened the laptop and sat down on the couch. He opened a folder which he had created earlier that day. It had multiple subfolders, and he opened the subfolders which were named as Silvio and Claudio. Mike opened the photographs in question and maximised it on the screen.

"I put the photos side by side, just check out the footprint. For me this is identical and I am open to any of you disagreeing." Mike said to the team as he had the pictures open.

"Next, there was a Trojan horse on all the phones of all the deceased, barring Vincenzo. There were four events, where all the deceased met Filippo. There is a very good chance the phones were infected with the virus during one of these events." Mike said further while the others were looking on intently with Matteo specifically looking more convinced of what Mike was saying.

"What next, Mike?" Matteo asked. The others looked at Mike with a questioning look in their eyes, eager to hear what he was about to say next.

"Claudio's murder, this is the kicker. It took less than two minutes, from the moment the killer had entered the cemetery, shot everyone and abducted Claudio. He made sure Claudio was dragged away before anyone could spot what had happened at the cemetery which, mind you, is in the same premises as the church close to two hundred metres away. This had to be done with precision and there had to be some sort of communication from inside, for someone to evade security and also not be accidentally spotted by anyone still in the vicinity" Mike added on, and everyone seemed to be convinced.

"But not the least, about seven years ago, independent blogger Pietro Rocco was found murdered in his own house, the case is still ongoing and the assassins are still wanted for armed robbery. I repeat armed robbery and murder. The article he wrote was questioning the activities of Filippo Patrizi, someone held in very high regard with a great standing in society. Pietro had written an article on his blog, in which he had stated that Claudio was taking advantage of immigrants and using their vulnerability and statelessness for organ trafficking. The article concluded with the final lines mentioning it's always easier to dispose of someone who doesn't even exist, which is the case of all the undocumented migrants who were being helped by Filippo's NGO as well. When the entire country was ravaged by covid, the orphanages under Filippo's control had a lot of cases and a lot of deaths, especially undocumented migrants. What if those that got reported were not natural deaths? What if he just used a national emergency for his advantage? I'm not saying he didn't do it before, I am just saying that he probably took it up a notch using the pandemic as an excuse. We had so many rumours over the years about him, again none of them could be proved. What if this guy and the deceased were all part of a circle and there was some issue which broke out between them? That he is targeting whoever he feels knows too much? At the end of the day, it all comes down to connections and power, maybe we're just stuck in one big power play at this point." Mike said to his team, with a stoic posture as he opened up all the documents and evidence he had put together in that folder and shared the files across to all of them.

"You know, with all the leads we had earlier, this link you established seems to be the one which we need to pursue. We need to act quick." Matteo said to Mike, rubbing his forehead while trying to think.

"How do we speak to Filippo?" Mario asked everyone.

"My advice is that we don't. We follow him, our contacts have said he is meeting Ernesto at 'Oceanhead', the nightclub near the beach tonight, we follow and try to find what they both are saying. If possible, bug them." Mike said to Mario, as the others looked on.

"Tonight?" Mario exclaimed, surprised at what Mike just said

"I know, right? it's a bit shady that they meet in a nightclub, which has a certain reputation as we all know over the years, right after Claudio's death? I'm starting to believe that they're there to enjoy the concert tonight. I believe, we might be able to find further evidence on Filippo, if we managed to bug into their conversation." Mike said to Mario as he looked at the entire team.

"So what's the play here boss, do you have any ideas?" Federico looked at Matteo, trying to find out if he had thought of something.

"Let's keep all this away from Domenico for now, to begin with. Next, Lorenzo, you're going to need a pretty good disguise to get into the VIP section as one of the waiters. Mario, I want you there, looking at communication and being our eyes on the club. Me and Federico, we will go in just for a drink and the concert and check who else is coming there tonight." Matteo said to Federico but also to the entire team.

"What about me?" Mike asked Matteo.

"You're staying put, get some proper dinner and stay in the house, resting. Just like the doctor's told you." Matteo said to Mike.

"Please tell me you're kidding?" Mike said to Matteo, surprised by what he had said.

"No Mike, I'm not, I don't want you in the field for the next two days, maybe it's about time you listened to at least what doctors tell you." Matteo told off Mike in a stern tone.

"If you really think that I'm going to stay at home, while you guys are out on the field tonight, good fucking luck. You can fire me right now, but I will still be there.

I'm staying with Mario in the MCV." Mike looked at Matteo, as he went to his room and got himself a shirt and a jean.

"Mike, there's already enough scrutiny on you and now the media are on your ass a bit, especially with you being at the cemetery in Claudio's murder, don't you get it?" Matteo said to Mike.

"If anything, I've already been demonised by the press a few times earlier, so one more time isn't going to make much of a difference. I am coming, whether you like it or not." Mike responded to Matteo.

" Mike, arghhhh, you know what, fuck it. I don't want you setting foot outside that truck, or I'll personally write your suspension order officially if I see you anywhere inside the club. Am I clear?" Matteo set to Mike.

"Fine, as long as there isn't a shootout, I'm inside the MCV all the time." Mike said to Matteo while changing his shirt.

The team started to prepare for the night for their next mission. At around 8PM, Filippo arrived at the club. Lorenzo was disguised as one of the waiters for the night around the VIP area with Matteo and Lorenzo mingling with the crowd at the concert. All of them were bugged with Mike and Mario keeping an eye out for them in the MCV, parked at a distance away from the sight of anyone.

10

The Nightclub Murders

"Get ready, Filippo just arrived. He has two bodyguards with him and he is centring the club." Mike said to the team.

"I see him." Matteo responded.

"Lorenzo, you're up, he sent it in the VIP area." Federico said.

"I see both of them, Ernesto is receiving Filippo." Lorenzo said.

Lorenzo went into the VIP area with a bottle of champagne and food. He dropped a plate of fries while keeping the food and drinks on the table. Irking the ire of Ernesto while Filippo remained expressionless and looked at Ernesto.

"You idiot, what do you have your eyes on top of your head like a frog?" Ernesto said to Lorenzo.

"Am so sorry sir, I am absolutely sorry. I just slipped, let me clean it up, am really really sorry." Lorenzo said while picking up the fries from the ground.

Without anyone noticing, Lorenzo had a very small microphone stuck to his glove, he was able to stick the microphone inside the VIP area, on the black walls, right behind the couch where Ernesto and Filippo were sitting, while cleaning up the floor of the fries before he left. The team were listening to the conversation between Filippo and Ernesto. Just Like Mike had predicted, they were talking about their previous murders and discussed a group of migrants being imprisoned in a mansion.

"I know, it's bad timing, but we need to complete the shipment this Saturday, so let's not delay the operation for any reason whatsoever." Filippo said to Ernesto.

"There shouldn't be a delay on that; it will be done at the said time." Ernesto replied.

"Coming to the next issue at hand. How many suspects do you have?" Filippo asked Ernesto.

"Quite a few boss, Claudio and Vincenzo, those idiots. They've ruffled too many feathers in their quest to get into the Parliament." Ernesto replied to Filippo.

"Let's put a hit on all of them, who do you suspect? I want them all gone. No more chances, we purge them all." Filippo said without any sort of stress, calm and composed.

"Understood, let me go downstairs and get some arrangements done." Ernesto said to Filippo, leaving the VIP area for a few minutes.

The club was eccentric that night due to the concert happening. Everyone in the crowd was dressed over the top while the band was playing their emo/goth rock music. Ernesto came downstairs while Matteo and Federico had their eyes on him while Lorenzo went into the VIP area and for another glass of champagne to Filippo and kept the bottle on the table while leaving again.

Ernesto in the meantime kept going towards the backstage area and was going through the crowd, followed by one of his guards. The crowd were all jumping and pushing. Matteo and the others had a bit of difficulty keeping an eye on Ernesto, when he went into the crowd. A few seconds later screaming was heard from the crowd, not from the songs played by the band, but as a result of Ernesto falling to his knees with blood pouring onto the floor, forming a red pool which made people close by immediately scream out. Ernesto had been stabbed by someone taking cover in the crowd, his lungs and one fatal strike at the heart. Matteo, Lorenzo and Federico rushed in the crowd and started searching for any suspects and club goers in panick started running outside the club. Mike jumped out of the MCV and ran towards the club. Filippo and his guards came down from the VIP area and his other guards outside ran into the club and surrounded him, forming a circle and making sure he was brought out in safety and into his limousine, before being driven away with his bodyguards right behind him. Mike ran into the club into the utter chaos of what was happening. Matteo, Federico and Lorenzo had no idea what had happened and how the killer got Ernesto. Even worse, they had missed him. He had gotten away using the chaos and none of them had an idea who it was. The eccentric dressing of the crowd played into his hands.

"Fucking great, he's pulled out the murder right under the noses of all of us." Federico burst out in anger.

"Mario, try to get the CCTV of this place, there should be something for us." Matteo said to Mario.

"You were on top, were you able to see something?" Mike asked Lorenzo.

"Nothing, this whole thing happened when I was in the VIP room, engaged with Filippo." Lorenzo responded to Mike

"Where did the sky learn his trade, even ninjas wouldn't be this stealthy." Mike responded in frustration.

The team spent the night looking for clues and investigating the club bartenders, patrons, the band and a few people from the crowd for any clues. Nothing concrete came out of anything for them that night even if they were there for the next few hours. The team left empty-handed, frustrated with themselves. All of them went home, angry and embarrassed at the same time. Mike and Matteo barely spoke to each other at home, with Matteo going directly to his room upstairs and Mike going to bed directly while keeping an eye on the news with social media playing a big part for him to learn current events.

Mike woke up around 9AM. and saw Matteo had already left the house. He turned on the TV and watched the news, the murder at Oceanhead. Turning point for all the news channels again. He switched it off and went to make a coffee when his phone rang. Mike answered the phone.

"Hello Captain Michelangelo, hope you had a good morning after a bad night." The voice on the phone said.

"Who the fuck are you?" Mike asked the person on the phone.

"Filippo Patrizi, does that help?" Filippo identified himself. "I think you need to cancel dinner at Rita's house for tonight and work on saving her life along with her daughter." Filippo added further.

"What the hell are you talking about?" Mike asked Filippo, shocked at what he heard.

"Just get dressed and go outside, get in the car without any questions, any deviation or else I'll send you the heads of both the girls for your dinner tonight. How does that sound?" Filippo said to Mike, in the same monotonous tone he had been speaking all along, as if he had done this a million times before.

Mike took a minute to compose himself after what just happened, but he did not have any time to waste. He got dressed quickly and ran outside the gate. He saw three men waiting with a car, the rear door open and them pointing towards the open door for Mike to get in. Mike walked towards them and got into the car which was waiting for him. The moment he got into the car one of the guys hit him with a needle at his neck while he had his back turned, making Mike unconscious. The next time Mike woke up he was sitting in a chair with Filippo sitting opposite him surrounded by his men.

"I hope the ride was not too bumpy, Mike." Filippo said to Mike, calmly.

"What the heck do you want from me, and where is Rita and her daughter?" Mike asked Filippo, sounding intense.

"Ohhh they're downstairs, along with a few people. Depending on what your answers are, I'll decide if they live or die or end up in a hospital bed with the capabilities of vegetables for the rest of their lives. It all depends on you, Captain Michelangelo Costa." Filippo's voice was cold and firm.

"You got the wrong guy, I don't even know what you want from me." Mike replied, countering Filippo.

Filippo simply smiled, got up from his chair and stepped close to Mike. He took his phone from his pocket and gave Mike's phone to him, asking him to call Federico, Lorenzo or Mario. Mike's face turned pale, mortified by the way Filippo had looked at him and asked him to dial his own colleagues. He frantically dialled his colleagues, but all of their phones were engaged, no one picked up the phones.

"No luck reaching them? That's sad. Check your phone now and you will get a few images." Filippo said to Mike. He was absolutely tied with Mike's emotions at this point.

Mike opened his messages and saw the SUV in which his colleagues normally travelled, was upside down with the driver's side almost completely smashed. It seemed to have been a major accident, but judging from a completely indifferent Filippo, who was checking his phone as if it was just like any other day, he knew too well it wasn't.

"Shall we talk now? Or do you still want to bullshit me, 'cause I can keep going next for Domenico, Matteo, Mariella pretty much even a dog which breathed the same air as you?" Filippo said to Mike.

"What do you want to know?" Mike asked Filippo, knowing he was out of options.

"Before I ask you something, I'll give you credit; I normally don't remember people like your father,

Giuseppe. But you made me remember him, find out about him, just so I know about you. It just didn't feel like coincidence when you and your buddies were present during all these murders. Got my attention to pull out every single detail of your histories and wala, what do I find? Your father worked in the orphanage which we burned down ourselves to destroy evidence. If my guess is right, you've been carrying that vengeance for close to three decades just to be even and avenge your father, haven't you? I am impressed Mike." Filippo said to Mike, who looked shocked that Filippo knew about his past and was trying to think of what he could even say next.

"Well, at least now you know why I want you dead and your empire destroyed, the people who think you're an angel should finally see you in your true colours, hell's messenger on Earth." Mike replied to Filippo defiantly.

"Good, now that we're on the same page, this person is our primary suspect for Ernesto's murder, my guess is that he is the one who murdered everyone associated with me. Somehow I feel, you know him. Can you tell me who the fuck he is?" Filippo showed a blurry picture to Mike, a man with long hair wearing eyeliners and earrings with the CCTV picking his image during the chaos of people running after the murder.

"You couldn't even get a decent picture? I don't think I could tell you even with a clear picture, let alone with this one." Mike replied to Filippo, who smacked him in his face with the back of his gun.

"You guys, can you please give him a treat him for a while, see if some massage solves his speech issues?" Filippo said to his guards in the room.

Mike was beaten black and blue for the next hour. Five men punching, kicking and hitting him with batons. Filippo came back into the room with a glass of champagne, another guard joined in and came inside the room. Mike could barely stand or move at this point, Filippo took his gun, the gun was pointed at the back of the head of Mike, while Filippo stood there taunting Mike with his helplessness.

"You really think you had all of this coming together finally, didn't you? Well, it could have and it almost did. But that's the difference between you and me, Michelangelo Costa. Difference between someone who is in law enforcement and someone who controls almost the entire crime syndicate in the country." Filippo kept taunting Mike, knocking him on his head.

"Yeah, I thought I did, now you got me, let Rita and her kid go. They don't have anything to do with all this." Mike said to Filippo as he kept staring at him.

"Cute, so cute. You don't hold the cards Mike; I'm going to cut them open, remove every internal organ I can put in a jar, rub it in your face and I'm going to show you how they died without any of their vital organs, their body just a shell. Then I'm going to do the same with you. With you? I only plan on keeping you alive until you tell me who else is involved in this with you? Who are your associates?! Give me the names, and maybe I will let that little girl survive and maybe put you and that woman to sleep with just one single bullet in your heads." Filippo asked Mike, shooting him on his left palm, Mike squirming and bringing his hands to his chest, while Filippo stood with a cold blank stare and a sly grin which could pass off as him genuinely being the Devil's associate on Earth.

Filippo then kicked Mike in the head making him fall down and stood on Mike's hand where he was shot, further torturing him for the answer he was looking for. A blast occurred outside of the mansion, which was heard from where everyone was standing. All their attention turned towards where the sound came from. When something rolled on the floor next to Filippo, Mike turned around, instantly covering his ears when the device which rode next to Filippo exploded into a powerful flashbang blinding everyone in the room. Five gunshots echoed next within a few seconds, Filippo saw five of his men fall down with headshots, and he turned around to notice one of the guards peeled off a face mask, showing the man behind the blurry face, which was picked up on the CCTV camera at the nightclub the previous night, during the murder of Ernesto. Filippo tried to shoot at the mysterious person, but then he was shot on both his shoulders and elbows making his arms completely useless.

Two more guards entered the other door who were also taken out by the mysterious person.

"You? Guards, Guards!!!!" Filippo was crying in pain while giving the impression he knew the shooter while calling for his men.

"Shut the fuck up and sit down, all of your men are dead." The shooter pulled a chair and forced Filippo on it and pushed the chair towards the wall. The guy had no emotions in his face and he stepped close to Mike.

"Are you ok?" The man asked Mike and held out his hand to help him.

"Couldn't you have done this a few minutes earlier?" Mike asked the shooter while Filippo was looking at both of them confused. The shooter turned towards Filippo and so did Mike.

"Reception problems for the bomb and the remote." The man responded to Mike.

"No fucking way it's you? Is that you? The one who I think you to be? Do you two understand who the hell I am?" Filippo cried in anger.

"You don't need to be a hysterical old man, it is who you think it is. Allow me to introduce myself. People in this business, including you, know me by my call sign "Priest', you my friend played a huge part in my creation, and we met a few years ago, when you didn't quite complete the job." The shooter identified himself.

"Priest? Fucking Priest? You were supposed to be dead; I've shot you and you fell off that cliff." Filippo looked perplexed looking at Priest.

"Yet I survived. Pretty good shots though, I still have your bullet marks on my chest, as a memory. That also proved to me that I underestimated you and had too much belief in my own capabilities, that I needed help. 'Cause by now I wasn't just interested in taking you down, I wanted your empire to crumble too. You are the Megalodon shark in the ocean, and I wanted to wipe you out of existence." Priest said to Filippo, matching the evil look he was giving earlier to Mike.

"Last time I shot you, you didn't finish your story. Since you're back after five years, I'm inclined to think that you have a huge problem with me. Since I don't have my gun, why don't you surprise me on what makes me so important to you. That one of the world's most wanted assassins wants me dead so badly, full of vengeance, that he joined forces with an Italian secret service official with the same goal." Filippo said to Priest, demanding an answer while making himself more comfortable on the chair.

Priest walked and crouched a few feet away from Filippo and started talking; Mike in the meantime sat up holding his bullet wound hand.

"My parents were undocumented migrants who landed in Catania. They ended up seeking asylum, with a three year old me by their side. We ended up staying at the refugee camp for a few months, before being approached to work in the agricultural fields in Southern Italy. Was it legal? I don't even know. All I know is being stuck in the fields for hours, days, weeks and months in the sun, in the rain and the cold. Sleeping on the ground, seeing your parents starving but trying to make you laugh just so misery doesn't hit a three year old kid growing up and trying to keep his spirits high. One fine day, the entire migrant workers, along with us, were taken from those fields to a different location. When I woke up, I was in an orphanage. I was told my parents were working in another place and would be back in a few days. Imagine my shock; I was only three years old. I accidentally wandered to an underground makeshift surgery room, where I found both my mum and dad in hospital beds, lifeless. The next thing I remember is a very sharp blow on my head, with blood from my skull washing the white floor." Priest said to Filippo, not looking away for even a second. Both of them locked eyes at each other for the entirety of the conversation.

"Catania, huh? Well, even if you mention the city, it's a bit hard to find who exactly you talk about as your parents. Do you even know how small that detail is for me to even fake an apology? Better chance of finding fish in a desert. Hahahahahaha." Filippo replied to Priest, showing no sign of remorse and an evil smile to boot.

"You know, if I didn't know you any better, I would have lunged forward and punched you but you would have avoided it, probably pulled my gun and shot me and Mike over there. But it's good to know you're still kicking until the last moment, looking for a way out." Priest responded to Filippo, grinning as if to indicate he could see every move Filippo was about to do.

"Before we continue the remaining story, how the fuck would you survive if your skull was bashed in? Apparently, it wasn't done properly from what I see. Should I feed this guy to the fishes for doing an incomplete job and me having to listen to you? How many years ago was this? How old are you? Twenty-eight? Thirty??" Filippo asked Priest, trying his best to throw him off-course, establishing mind games looking for an opening in which he could make his move.

"Say this is where it gets interesting, the person who crashed my skull was you. I remembered your sick face back then; thirty years later I still see the same sick face sitting right before me. Time flies, huh motherfucker? Since you don't remember which place my parents could have been. I could probably tell you the day, because you left me to die. You proceeded to burn down that orphanage to cover the tracks off your illegal organ smuggling ring. I survived, which is a rather unfortunate circumstance for you, but a lot of people didn't, just like Mike's dad that night. You know sins catch up eventually, how does it feel that the sins you committed that night created two guys with a single thought in their head: your death. Removing the mask which you had so carefully placed on your face to show to the entire world. Bringing down your empire piece by piece, brick by brick." Priest said to Filippo, rubbing his chin while tapping the pistol he held on his legs. He was giving the vibe of a person who has not let his opponents words throw him off guard, two bulls charging at each other except one was a matador.

Final

The Alpha and the Omega

"What are you waiting for? Go ahead, shoot me, get it over with." Filippo said to Priest, goading him to end this life.

"You really think that after all these years, with two people planning whatever happened in this past week with vengeance close to thirty years to boot, you're going to die with one single shot to the head? Really?" Mike got up from the floor, looking at Filippo standing next to Priest.

"What?" Filippo asked, a bit perplexed, seeing his idea of a quick death was being rejected.

Priest ended up shooting him on his lungs, liver and kidneys and gave Mike a knife he had in his pants. Filippo was alive but struggling to breathe, Mike proceeded to stab Filippo right on his aorta, leaving him struggling to breathe even further, but also prolonging his death at the same time. Police sirens started coming into the earshot of both Priest and Mike.

“Mike, go find Rita and her kid and get the fuck outta here and live your life, this is the end of the road for us, I fear. Thank you for everything.” Priest said to Mike and gave him a hug.

Mike went outside the room while Priest waved goodbye to the dying Filippo. He took out an incendiary grenade and threw it next to Filippo and ran through the other entrance and disappeared out of sight, with the room engulfing in flames as Filippo screamed, death flashing before his eyes. Mike went to the next room and went down the stairs which lead to the cells downstairs. He shot at the lock, but could not open it easily and started to kick the door open, which it eventually gave in. He brought out Rita who held her daughter close to herself and proceeded to the next cells. He was able to see people locked in their cells crying for help. Mike told them he will be back with help and to hold on for a few more minutes. He helped Rita to walk up the stairs along with her daughter. The SWAT team had arrived by then with Matteo leading them to the mansion. Some of them came to Mike, Rita and her daughter and quickly took them outside to the medical personnel waiting for them. Mike told them about the underground stairway and the team rushed downstairs to save all the people who were locked up. All the people were led out safely and into waiting ambulances, receiving first aid. Almost all of them, with gratitude in their eyes, whenever Mike turned towards their line of sight. The SWAT team was making sure to put out the fire in the room where all the bodies were still burning along with the furniture. It took a few minutes for them to completely put it out because the fire had spread rapidly, fuelled by a gas leak as well. Matteo went inside the hall where he saw the charred bodies of Filippo and his men. He examined the room and saw only carnage, all the bodies were burned and the entire place was a fiery dungeon, even if the flames were out. The heat and the smell of the burned bodies filled the air in the room.

Matteo came outside the room and walked out the door; he saw Rita and her daughter put on a stretcher and being loaded inside an ambulance. Mike stood outside the vehicle while medical personnel put bandages on his arm. When the door was about to be closed, Mike said something to Rita and waved them off. Matteo waited for this moment and made his way to Mike, who was sitting in another ambulance nearby.

"Are you ok? How do you feel?" Matteo asked Mike, making sure he was ok.

"Clean exit for the bullet in my hand, so that's good. I just feel a bit banged up. Regarding you telling me yesterday about the suspension; I think I'm going to take a few days off if that's ok. This time around I will listen to the doctors and you." Mike responded to Matteo, being sarcastic at the end.

"That's fine, how did you manage to burn down that place though?" Matteo asked Mike, trying to understand what happened.

"Well, he wanted me to rat out our informers who did us a favour, so he could personally go on a purge. This is why I got all the bruises, the beatings and the bullet wound. He was basically saying that he was going to remove every vital organ from Rita and me as well, if I don't give up the names and also mention whatever we had found out in this investigation for the past year. In short, I don't know if he figured we were running a parallel secret investigation or he just assumed we had details because his gang was entirely wiped out. He also wanted details of whatever we found out on his organ trafficking and human trafficking business." Mike said to Matteo while having a sip of water.

"Moreover, on how I managed to escape, I was able to grab a gun from one of the guards, while they were distracted with the blast outside. I was able to use a human shield and took them out. Filippo did try to overpower me while trying to restrain him, so I could bring him in alive. But I had to shoot him to subdue, even when injured and disabled mostly. He still came back with a knife, but I was able to overpower him and stab him in his chest. I had no choice, I couldn't do anything. He pulled a grenade and threw it in the hall, he was defiant till the end. I believe it's incendiary, the grenade, pretty much engulfed the place in flames. Guess, he preferred to go out on his own terms than live with his true self exposed." Mike said to Matteo who was listening to him intently, while hearing his version of events.

"You are safe, Rita and her daughter are safe. That's all that matters." Matteo said to Mike, making sure he was relaxing.

"Yeah, I'm lucky something triggered an explosion on his limousine; although, it would have been even better if it had exploded a few minutes ago. I am curious what caused that explosion." Mike said to Matteo while looking at the remains of the limousine.

"How are the boys, are they going to be ok?" Mike asked Matteo, hoping for some good news on their condition.

"Federico is critical, Lorenzo and Mario are still in ICU, but they should be ok. You should go to the hospital as well Mike, let's hope for the best regarding our boys. I'll finish up here, maybe we'll know more about what caused that explosion, that's for another time, you endured a lot already, take it easy." Matteo responded to Mike.

"Take him, get him cleaned up properly." Matteo said to the emergency personnel treating Mike, who proceeded to help Mike inside the ambulance and took him to the hospital.

While in the ambulance, Mike was thinking about everything which had happened since the fateful day when his dad died as a victim of arson, his childhood in the orphanage. He remembered how Priest had reached out to him a year ago, a former wanted assassin, who was supposedly dead resurfaced, with the same goal as he had. To bring down the entire gang behind the murder of their parents. He was reminiscing the sequences where they decided the best way to take the entire empire of Filippo was to work together, one on the inside and one on the outside, a ghost, who did not even exist, executing the murders with pinpoint precision and planning. Every event planned and every outcome analysed for a specific reaction, with Mike taking the key role in throwing the investigation off-course wherever he could to keep Priest's existence a secret. Priest targeting Vincenzo first, to start the chain reaction of Claudio and the others at crossroads. With Silvio's murder pitting Alessio and the others to suspect each other. Mike and Priest decided that the entire gang should be taken out within a few days, where there was no time to regroup for the deceased, taking advantage of their confusion and their suspicion of each other. Mike's role was simple, he only had to support this ghost; he did not even have Priest's original name on record. Priest in return, executed the murders. A perfect ending to the plan which had involved a lot of sacrifices, but at the end, the result is all that mattered. Mike felt content, finally, after years of tormenting himself. He was able to have a sense of satisfaction. The impossible had been achieved, everyone involved in that empire stood like a Christmas tree with lights. Anyone remotely connected with all of the deceased, were in the spotlight. Every known criminal, big or small will be looked into. The country will go through a mass cleansing. Mike fell into unconsciousness while thinking about all this, his wounds finally taking their toll on his body but not on his heart.

Two weeks Later, the country was loud with news running in the background of multiple sting operations being conducted at various properties belonging to the Trentino's, several politicians, socialites, gang members based on the investigation of Mike and his colleagues. Federico was being woken up from his sleep.

"Hey, hey, wake up you lazy ass, staying in a hospital bed doesn't mean you have to be like a goddamn panda you dick!" Mike was trying to wake up Federico, surrounded by his team.

"How do you feel Alfred? Think you might pull through? I am going to need my driver back soon. Since I am missing the precinct" Mike said to Federico as the others were laughing in the background with Federico giving a smile even if he was in pain.

"Fuck you Mike, help me sit up" Federico said as he was trying to get up, Mike and Lorenzo went over his bedside and made sure Federico was able to sit up, with them cranking the bed a bit more higher on his upper body.

"How do you feel? You seem in high spirits, for someone who got shot and being brutally thrashed by five to six guys." Federico said to Mike, who still had a bandage on his arm and his head, like a bandana.

"I feel ok enough to make sure your ass is setup properly in bed, I got this discharged a week ago you idiot, remember?" Mike laughed at Federico.

"I am still surprised, that this team, which consists of personnel like all of you in this room was able to pull off this investigation successfully." A voice came from the back, Domenico stood at the entrance, looking at all of them.

"Good Morning Sir" the team greeted him in unison as Domenico made his way to the room.

"You boys did a fine job, all jokes aside. What you all pulled in the past two years is nothing short of a miracle. Especially you Mike, what you did all alone during your confrontation with Filippo, ensuring the safety of the hostages was indeed impressive. Good Work." Domenico said to Mike and the others, while shaking Mike's hands.

"This case has moved your reputations more than you can imagine, all of you will see that take effect in the upcoming days, but for now, enjoy the rest and get better, you all need it." Domenico said to the team.

Mike got a text message from Rita and he turned around a bit to hide his phone and started texting her back. Matteo, though, who saw Mike was texting her, came closer to him and whispered into his ears.

“Get out of here before your ex father-in-law finds out about that girl and your potential dinner date with her today.” Matteo said to Mike, who nodded back.

“I have some work to do and pick up a package, you all proceed, I'll see you all later, I really need to run.” Mike said to the team as he turned around and left the room, the others looking on and continuing to talk among themselves.

Mike got into his car and started driving to Rita's workplace to pick her up for dinner. He was driving slowly through the crazy Neapolitan traffic, with almost the entire city finishing work at the same time. He was still able to arrive on time though; she had texted him that she would need to finish up some work. Mike took his phone and opened his online game putting on his headphones, when his phone started to ring. Mike answered the phone call and it came from a private number.

"How are you? Captain Michelangelo Costa." The voice said over the phone, which Mike instantly realised was Priest.

"All good, waiting to pick up my date. How about you? Hopefully you haven't started picking up assassination contracts again." Mike said to Priest, looking around the buildings and surrounding streets nearby.

"She seemed nice, I'm pretty sure you're lucky. Assassination contracts? No, still figuring out what to do next, you can stop looking around trying to see if I am nearby Mike, I am not near you or even in Naples." Priest responded to Mike.

"Yeah she's a great girl. How do you know I was looking around and hey, can I ask you something then? Where are you?" Mike asked Priest.

"Just a lucky guess you were looking around. Somewhere close by to Italy, on a tall building looking at the city." Priest responded to Mike, keeping his location a mystery which baffled Mike.

"Ok, I'm going to stop asking personal questions, mystery man. I don't know whether it's you in general or you got a serious case of trust issues man. Even after what we pulled together." Mike said to Priest, trying to figure him out.

"I just wanted to call you and thank you again for your help for our plan earlier Mike. I couldn't have done all that without your help." Priest said to Mike, sitting on a wall.

"Likewise, I couldn't have done whatever I wanted to do without your help, I can finally sleep well, hopefully you too. Knowing the filths who were responsible for so much pain. Not for just you and me, but thousands are no more. It's a shame you don't get the credit you deserve for helping this country and even this continent as a whole." Mike said to Priest.

"Mental satisfaction and your heart finally at peace is more valuable than praise and recognition Mike, I finally have that. Maybe that's why I don't know what to do next and hence need to figure out where my life takes me further. 'Cause I've never felt this way before, it's new, exciting and scary at the same time. Funny that peace makes me scared, haha" Priest responded to Mike with a certain indifference but turning to hope at the end.

"I hear you, it's just a shame that I still don't know your name. I am still surprised on how and why you thought it was a good idea to approach me earlier, what if i had refused to help? With this in mind, I can understand why you keep your secret though, you came as a ghost and you leave as a ghost." Mike said to Priest laughing over the phone.

"You can't really be a gun for hire without reading people's intentions Mike, then again, I still stand by what I said, all my contract kills, were people who deserved to go either way. I live by a code even if it is on the wrong side of the law" Priest said to Mike, smiling."

"Live your life Captain, you deserve good things in your life, Godspeed!" Priest said to Mike and was about to disconnect the call, when Mike started speaking.

"Hey Priest! Hold on a second, you said you're trying to figure out your life and you actually have no idea what to do next. Put it this way, you're starting completely new. That's all that matters right now. You are the Alpha and the Omega of your own life, not a lot of people get that chance in a lifetime, you're one of the lucky ones. Take this as a blessing. Maybe you'll get used to it and start enjoying it as well. Take care of yourself." Mike said to Priest, who this time around didn't let Mike disconnect the phone.

"Mike, before you go, I need to tell you something." Priest said to Mike, clicking his tongue.

"My real name is Nate. I am somewhere around the Danube river looking at it flow majestically in the moonlight, I love this river. Anyways, I might keep moving around the continent for a while." Priest said while revealing his name and giving his location vaguely.

"Woww, I wonder how much convincing you did to yourself to say that. So is Nate for Nathaniel, Nathan or even Natalie? All jokes aside, maybe this means the end of the name Priest once and for all." Mike joked to Nate while popping a chewing gum into his mouth.

"Nate could also be for nature? That's all you get from me Captain. With regards to your fear of me going back to my former life? Priest is dead and he will always remain dead, unless someone digs him out. So you don't need to worry about me going down that road again. Next time we run into each other, if we ever, you can call me Nate. Not a lot of people call or called me that before too much. Enjoy your date Captain Mike, like i said earlier, Godspeed!" Nate disconnected the call as he stood up and watched the city of Budapest, from the castle walls while turning around and walking away. Mike got out of the car and turned around to see Rita arrive from her office, smiling at him as she came towards him.

Both Mike and Nate hoped to have a fresh start in life, away from chaos finally as they both looked at the sky and the full moon gracing the night.

Three Weeks Later, a man walks over to Emmanuel Trentino who was watching the news on the television, with various politicians calling for his resignation and dismissal from the Italian Parliament. In light of the recent investigations brought by the case handled by Michelangelo Costa and his team.

"This is the man who we suspect was behind the murders in the nightclub." The man kept a photo of Nate from the side as he was exiting the club, his face covered by paint and accessories.

"Find out who this is and find out the details of everyone who was handling this case." Emmanuel looked at the man, while he took the photo of Nate in his hands to give a closer look.

About the Author

A.M.Freitas, grew up in Pondicherry, South India having an intense passion for arts since childhood. He started writing for independent projects which eventually led to his first book, "Kensington – Once Burned Twice Thy Pain – Part One" in 2018, the same year he left India to settle down in Europe. He decided to continue publishing his other projects further as a book which led to "THE FOOTPRINT"

www.ingramcontent.com/pod-product-compliance
Lightning Source LLC
La Vergne TN
LVHW041206150826
845673LV00001B/297

* 9 7 9 8 8 8 9 7 5 5 2 9 6 *